The Road to Mecca

A DRAMA IN TWO ACTS

by Athol Fugard

Suggested by the life and work of
Helen Martins of New Bethesda

SAMUEL FRENCH, INC.
45 WEST 25TH STREET   NEW YORK 10010
7623 SUNSET BOULEVARD   HOLLYWOOD 90046
LONDON   *TORONTO*

ISBN 0 573 66018 2   Printed in U.S.A.

FOR S.H.

The soul selects her own society—
Then—shuts the door—
On her divine majority—
Present no more.

— Emily Dickinson

A NOTE
ON
MISS HELEN

ATHOL FUGARD

It was a drive into the Karoo to spend a holiday on a friend's farm and the route I drove that took me for the first time through what had only been a name on a map until then: New Bethesda, a small village in what turned out to be an absolutely magnificent setting. As I drove through it, I couldn't help responding to it, because I was actually born in that part of the world — as a matter of fact, I was born fifteen miles away from New Bethesda in a place called Middelburg. Driving to my friend's farm I was struck by its isolation and thought to myself, hell, this would be quite a nice place to have a house to escape from the city if ever I felt like getting away from the world. I mentioned this to my friend, who said, "Well, you know, the houses are dirt-cheap in New Bethesda because there has been a move from the rural areas into the cities. You could pick up a house there very cheaply." So on the way back to Port Elizabeth, I stopped and looked around, and I discovered there were houses for sale very, very cheaply.

I returned three months later with the express purpose of buying a house, which I still own. In the course of looking at various houses and getting to know a few of the locals, reference was made to a rather strange character who lived in the village. Her name was Helen Martins and the people were kind of apologetic about her because they regarded her as a little crazy. They said that her craziness took the form of rather silly statues and sculpture that she made and had all around her house. I obviously couldn't resist the temptation of strolling in the direction of her house and seeing Miss Helen's "Mecca" for the first time. She was still alive at that point but had become virtually a total recluse. So, apart from seeing her in the distance once or twice, and nodding at her when she was among her statues and I happened to be walking past, I never got to know her personally.

About two years after I bought my house and started visiting the village regularly, Miss Helen committed suicide. Obviously, as a writer I couldn't help responding to this very eccentric character in this strange little community — a community which was in a sense hostile to her life and her work because it was a deviation from what the townspeople considered to be the way a life should be lived — and thinking: there's a damn good story. Over the next few years thoughts about Miss Helen occurred with some frequency in my notebooks.

I also began to discover more about the real Miss Helen. For example, up until the age of fifty, when her husband died, there was nothing about her that gave any hint of what was going to happen. Then her life suddenly erupted in this remarkable way in terms of her sculpture. Suddenly there was the first statue in the garden, and then over the next fifteen or seventeen years she worked away, with obsessive dedication, at what must have been a personal vision. After her death I went on to discover what she had done inside her house as well — as remarkable a feat as what she had done outside with the sculptures. Those seventeen years of creative activity ended, and there was a period of about eighteen months or two years during which she made nothing, did nothing and became very paranoid, very depressed. One night she killed herself by drinking caustic soda (the Americans would call it lye): she burned away her insides.

7

Though obviously in a sense provoked by Miss Helen's story, I'd never quite been hooked by it. I'm a fisherman and I know the difference between a fish that's just playing with your bait and one that says "WRITE! I'M IT!" and takes your rod down as you sit back and put the hook deep in. I wasn't hooked.

The hooking came through a coincidence of factors. At a personal level, I began to realize, a provocation had been thrown at me four years previously by an actress who was doing *A Lesson from Aloes* in Amsterdam (she had also done *Boesman and Lena*). In the course of a conversation at the Rijksmuseum she said to me, "Those are marvellous roles you have created for women. I'm very grateful to you for that but, looking back at your work, I can't help being struck by the fact that you have never had two women together. When are you going to do that?" And I suddenly registered for the first time that although I had created an interesting gallery of women's portraits over the years, I'd never put two women together on a stage as the focus of the whole event. Other personal factors in my life helped give the provocation more of an edge, more of a demand that I think about it and try to do something about it.

While this was happening to me, I discovered another fact about Miss Helen: that in the last years of her life, the last period of nothing until her death, there had been one very significant friendship — a friendship with a young woman, a social worker from Cape Town. I'd rather not mention her name, because I've taken every liberty I felt necessary in writing the play. I've done my own thing; I've not written a documentary. I discovered the friendship had been very, very meaningful. I accidentally happened to meet the young woman. I was struck by her because she was very strong, a very remarkable person with a strong social conscience, a strong sense of what South Africa was about, a strong outrage at what was wrong with it. I couldn't help thinking of the anomaly of this sort of stern decency encountering the almost feudal world of New Bethesda — a South Africa which disappeared from the rest of the country a hundred years ago. Obviously, that young person had quite a confrontation with the village.

Because of my respect for Miss Helen the young woman gave me, as a gesture, a little memento of the occasion when we met — a photograph of herself and Miss Helen. I took one look at the photograph — it's a brilliant, beautiful photograph — and there was the play. There was the coincidence. I was hooked. That was the moment when I swallowed the bait.

From an interview conducted by Gitta Honegger and Rassami Patipatpaopong first published in Theater magazine

PROMENADE THEATRE

Under the direction of Ben Sprecher

Stephen   Jujamcyn   Jonathan
Graham   Theatres   Farkas

Norma & David   Maurice Rosenfield &
Langworthy   Lois F. Rosenfield, Inc.

In association with

James B. Freydberg & Max Weitzenhoffer

present

YVONNE BRYCELAND   ATHOL FUGARD

AMY IRVING

in

THE ROAD TO MECCA

Written and Directed by **ATHOL FUGARD**

Set Design by   Costume Design by   Lighting Design by
John Lee Beatty   **Susan Hilferty**   **Dennis Parichy**

Casting Consultants   Associate Producers
Meg Simon/Fran Kumin   **Robin Ullman & Stuart Thompson**

Originally produced by Yale Repertory Theatre, Lloyd Richards, Artistic Director

The Producers wish to express their appreciation to Theatre
Development Fund for its support of this production

10

CAST

(in order of appearance)

Miss Helen . . . . YVONNE BRYCELAND

Elsa Barlow . . . . AMY IRVING

Marius Byleveld . . . . ATHOL FUGARD

The action takes place in the small Karoo village of
New Bethesda, South Africa.

THERE WILL BE ONE FIFTEEN-MINUTE INTERMISSION.

11

CHARACTERS

MISS HELEN
ELSA BARLOW
MARIUS BYLEVELD

TIME: Autumn 1974.

PLACE: The home of Miss Helen in a small village in the Great Karoo, a semi-desert region in the center of South Africa.

The Road to Mecca

ACT I

Scene: (The lounge, and leading-off it a bedroom alcove, of a house in the small Karoo village of New Bethesda. An extraordinary room by virtue of the attempt to use as much light and color as was humanly possible. The walls, mirrors on all of them, are all of different colors while on the ceiling and floor are solid, multi-colored geometric patterns. The final effect however is not bizarre but rather one of light and extravagant fantasy. Just what the room is really about will be revealed later when its candles and lamps, again a multitude of them of every size, shape and color, are lit. The late afternoon LIGHT does give some hint though of the magic to come. There is a hallway in the back with doors leading to two back rooms and a kitchen. There are large windows in the back rooms and seen through them the backyard . . . Miss Helen's "Mecca" crowded with its collection of strange statues.

AT RISE: MISS HELEN is in the bedroom alcove. A frail, bird-like little woman in her late sixties. A suggestion of personal neglect, particularly in her clothes which are shabby and were put on with obvious indifference to the final effect. She is nervously fussing around an old-style washstand laying out a towel, washcloth, soap and a robe. MISS HELEN then checks the kettle in the kitchen, runs into the lounge, picks up the blanket and pillow from the chaise and throws them into the back room. SHE picks up the overnight bag, briefcase and sweater and drags them

13

into the bedroom alcove. MISS HELEN runs to the table, puts all her papers into the red box and quickly shuts it. SHE scurries into the hallway directing her attention to the front door. ELSA enters through it. A strong young woman wearing sweaty travel clothes and sunglasses.)

ELSA. Not cold enough yet for the car to freeze up, is it?

HELEN. No. No danger of that. We haven't had any frost yet.

ELSA. I've just pulled it off the road. I'm too exhausted to put it away. (*Collapses in a chair and throws her keys and sunglasses onto the table. MISS HELEN pours her a glass of water.*) Whew! Thank God that's over. Another hour and I would have been wiped out. That road gets longer and longer every time.

HELEN. Your hot water is nearly ready.

ELSA. Good. (*Starts to unpack her overnight bag.*)

HELEN. (*Holding up the box of soaps.*) Nice clean towels . . . and I've opened that box of scented soaps you brought me last time.

ELSA. (*Laying out her toiletries on the washstand.*) What? Oh those. Haven't you used them yet?

HELEN. Of course not! I was keeping them for a special occasion.

ELSA. And this is it?

HELEN. Yes. An unexpected visit from you is a very special occasion. Is that all your luggage?

ELSA. When I said a short visit I really meant it.

HELEN. Such a long way to drive for just one night.

ELSA. I know.

HELEN. You don't think you could . . . ?

ELSA. Stay longer?

HELEN. Maybe two nights?

ELSA. Impossible. We're right in the middle of exams. I've got to be back in that classroom at eight-thirty on Monday morning. As it is I should have been sitting at home right now marking papers. I even brought a pile of them with me just in case I get a chance up here. (*Starts to undress . . . first the shoes.*)

HELEN. Put anything you want washed on one side and I'll get a message to Katrina first thing in the morning.

ELSA. Don't bother her with that. I can do it myself.

HELEN. (*Takes a pillow from the chaise and props it behind ELSA's back.*) You can't leave without seeing Katrina. She'll never forgive me if I didn't let her know you're here. Please . . . even if it's just for a few minutes.

ELSA. I won't leave without seeing Katrina, Miss Helen! But I don't need her to wash a pair of pants and a bra for me. I do my own washing. (*Takes off her blouse, then her tank top.*)

HELEN. I'm sorry . . . I just thought you might . . . there's an empty drawer here if you want to pack anything away.

ELSA. (*An edge to her voice.*) Please stop fussing, Miss Helen! I know my way around by now.

HELEN. It's just that if I'd known you were coming I would have had everything ready for you.

(*Continues to tidy up the room . . . puts the drawer back into the sideboard, throws her cardigan and some old rags in the back room, then clears the dirty tea cup from the shaker table.*)

ELSA. Everything is fine just the way it is.

HELEN. No it isn't! I don't even know that I've got enough in the kitchen for a decent supper tonight. I did buy bread yesterday, but for the rest . . .

ELSA. Please Miss Helen! If we need anything I'll get old Retief to open his shop for us. In any case I'm not hungry. All I need at this moment is a good wash and a chance to unwind so that I can forget I've been sitting in a motorcar for twelve hours. (*Pours cold water from the jug into the basin.*)

HELEN. Be patient with me Elsie. Remember the little saying, patience is a virtue, virtue is a grace. Grace is a little . . .

ELSA. (*Unexpectedly sharp.*) For God's sake, Helen! Will you leave me alone for one moment, please! (*Pause.*)

HELEN. (*Timidly.*) I'll see about your hot water.

(*Goes into the kitchen. ELSA slumps down on the bed, head in her hands. MISS HELEN returns a few seconds later with a large kettle of hot water. SHE handles it with difficulty.*)

ELSA. Let me do that!

(*SHE jumps up and takes the kettle away from MISS HELEN. The two WOMEN stand staring at each other for a few seconds. ELSA puts down the kettle then puts her hands on MISS HELEN's shoulders.*)

HELEN. I've got the small one on for tea.

ELSA. My turn to say sorry.

HELEN. No need for that.

ELSA. Please! It will help. Sorry Miss Helen. I also need to hear you say you forgive me.

HELEN. To tell you the truth I was also getting on my nerves.

ELSA. (*Now smiling.*) Come on.

HELEN. Oh alright . . . but I promise you it isn't necessary. You're forgiven.

ELSA. (*Leading MISS HELEN over to a chair.*) Now sit down and stop worrying about me. We're both going to close our eyes, take a deep breath and start again. Ready?

HELEN. Ready.

ELSA. One, two, three . . . (*Closed eyes and deep breaths, THEY collapse into laughter.*) And now?

HELEN. (*Sly, tongue-in-cheek humor we will come to recognize as characteristic of the relaxed MISS HELEN.*) Well, if you really mean it, I think the best thing is for you to get back into your car, drive around the block and arrive again. And this time, I want you please to hoot three times the way you usually do so that I don't think a ghost has walked in through the front door when you appear.

ELSA. (*Calling MISS HELEN's bluff.*) Right. Where are the car keys.

(*Finds them and heads for the front door.*)

HELEN. Where are you going?

ELSA. Do what you said. Drive around the block and arrive again.

HELEN. Like that?

ELSA. Why, what's wrong?

HELEN. Elsie! Sterling Retief will have a heart attack if he sees you like that.

ELSA. But I wear less than this when I go to the beach.

(*Ignoring MISS HELEN's protests, SHE hurries out of the front door.*)

HELEN. (*Running after ELSA.*) Elsie, Elsie, Elsie, I was only playing the fool!

(*ELSA hurries around outside and re-enters through the kitchen. SHE revs up her motorcar, grinds through all its gears and "arrives." Three blasts on the HORN. The two WOMEN play the "arrival game" [specifics to be determined in rehearsal]. At the end of it THEY come together in a good laugh.*)

ELSA. God, if my friends in Cape Town could have seen that! You must understand, Miss Helen, Elsa Barlow is known as a "serious young woman." Bit of a blue-stocking in fact. Not much fun there! (*THEY sit at the table.*) I don't know how you did it, Helen, but you caught me with those stockings down from the first day we met. You have the rare distinction of being the only person who could make me make a fool of myself . . . and enjoy it.

HELEN. You didn't make a fool of yourself. And anyway what about me? Nearly seventy and behaving as if I were seven!

ELSA. Let's face it, there's a little girl hidden away in both of us.

HELEN. And they like to play together.

ELSA. Mine hasn't done that for a long time.

HELEN. And I didn't even know that mine was still alive.

ELSA. *That* she most certainly is. She's the one who comes running out to play first. Feeling better? (*Holds MISS HELEN's hands.*)

HELEN. Much better.

(*For the moment all tensions are gone. ELSA takes on cleaning herself as thoroughly as a basin of water, wash cloth and bar of scented soup will allow.*)

ELSA. (*Pours some hot water from the kettle into the basin.*) God, this Karoo dust gets right into your pores. I can even taste it. That first mouthful of tea will be mud. I'll fill up all the kettles tomorrow and have a really good scrub. When did you last have one? (*MISS HELEN has to think about it.*) Well, that settles it. Your name is down for one as well. (*A few seconds of industrious scrubbing. MISS HELEN watches her.*) What are you thinking?

HELEN. So many things! About the way you arrived just now. I wasn't joking. I really did think I was seeing a ghost. I heard the front door open . . . I thought that must be Katrina, because she also never knocks . . . but instead, there you were. (*SHE wants to say more but stops herself.*)

ELSA. Go on.

HELEN. It was so strange. Almost as if you didn't see me or anything else at first . . . didn't really want to. And so cross! I've never seen you like that before.

ELSA. (*Begins to dry herself.*) This isn't quite like the other times Miss Helen.

HELEN. That's a pity. They were all good times. (*Pause.*) So what sort of time is this going to be? A bad one?

ELSA. (*Evenly.*) I hope not. Doesn't have to be. That depends on you. (*MISS HELEN avoids Elsa's eyes. The YOUNG WOMAN looks around the room.*) But you're right. I hadn't really arrived until now.

HELEN. Where were you, Elsie?

ELSA. (*Thinks about the question before answering.*) Where was I? Way back at the turn-off to the village from the National Road — or maybe a few miles further along it now — walking to Cradock.

HELEN. I don't understand.

ELSA. (*Takes off her trousers, leaves them on the floor, then puts on the robe.*) I gave a lift to a woman outside Graaff-Reinet. I dropped her at the turn-off to the village. That's most probably where she is now.

HELEN. Who was she?

ELSA. (*Shrugging her shoulders.*) An African woman.

HELEN. Cradock! That's a long walk.

ELSA. I know.

HELEN. It's about another eighty miles from the turn-off.

(*SHE waits for Elsa to say more.*)

ELSA. (*Lays out the towel on the stool and begins to wash her feet.*) I nearly didn't stop for her. She didn't sign that she wanted a lift or anything like that. Didn't even look up when I passed by . . . I was watching her in the rear-view mirror. Maybe that's what told me there was a long walk ahead of her . . . the way she had her head down and just kept on walking. And then the baby on her back. It was hot out there, Miss Helen, hot and dry and a lot of empty space . . . not a farm-house in sight. She looked very small and unimportant in the middle of all that. Anyway I stopped the car and reversed and offered her a lift. Not very graciously. I'd already been driving for ten hours and all I wanted was to get here as fast as I could. Anyway, she got in and after a few miles we started talking. (*Pauses from her washing.*) Her English wasn't very good but when I finally got around to understanding what she was trying to tell me it added up to a good old South African story. Her husband, a farm laborer, had died recently and no sooner had they buried him when the "Baas" told her to pack-up and leave the farm. (*Dries her feet.*) So there she was . . . on her way to the Cradock district hoping to find a few distant relatives and a place to live. (*Trying to remember the woman as clearly as possible.*) About my age. The baby couldn't have been more than a few months old. All she had with her was one of those plastic shopping-bags they put your groceries in at supermarkets. I saw a pair of old slippers. She was barefoot.

HELEN. Poor woman.

ELSA. So I dropped her at the turn-off. Gave her what was left of my food and some money. She carried on walking and I drove here. (*A pause as SHE dumps the basin of water in the kitchen.*)

HELEN. Is there something else?

ELSA. No. That's all.

HELEN. I'm sure somebody else will give her a lift.

ELSA. (*Too easily.*) Hope so. Otherwise she and her baby are in for a night beside the road. There's eighty miles of the Karoo ahead of her. Shadows were already stretching out across the veld when she got out of the car. (*Puts on some face cream.*) The Great Karoo! And just when I thought I was getting used to it, beginning to like it in fact. Down in Cape Town I've actually caught myself talking rubbish about its vast space and emptiness, its awesome stillness and silence! Just like old Gertruida down the road. It's that alright, but only because everything else has been all but damned out of existence. It's so easy to see where you Afrikaners get your idea of God from. Beats me how you've put up with it so long, Miss Helen. Nearly seventy years? My God, you deserve a

medal. I would have packed-up and left it at the first
opportunity . . . let's face it, you've had plenty of
those.

HELEN. I was born here Elsa.

ELSA. I sympathize, Miss Helen. Believe me I truly
sympathize.

HELEN. It's not really as bad as you make it sound.
The few times I've been away I've always ended up missing it and longing to be back.

ELSA. Because you wanted to get back to your work.

HELEN. (*Shaking her head.*) No. Even before all that
started. It grows on you Elsa.

ELSA. (*Leaning on a chair.*) Which is just about all the
growing it seems to allow. For the rest it's as merciless as
the religion they preach around here. Looking out of the
car window this afternoon I think I finally understood a
few things about you Afrikaners . . . and it left me feeling just a little uneasy.

HELEN. You include me in all you're saying.

ELSA. Yes. You're still an Afrikaner, Miss Helen. You
were in there with them singing hymns every Sunday for
a long, long time. Bit of a renegade now I admit, but
you're still one at heart.

HELEN. And that heart is merciless? (*Pause.*)

ELSA. (*Sits in the chair and takes Miss Helen's hand.
The fatigue is still with her.*) No. That you aren't. A lot of
other things maybe, but certainly not that. Sorry, sorry,
sorry . . .

HELEN. You're still very cross, aren't you? And something else as well. There's a new sound in your voice. One
I never heard before.

ELSA. What are you talking about?

HELEN. Like the way you talked about that woman on
the road. Almost as if you didn't care, which I know isn't
true.

ELSA. Of course I cared. I cared enough to stop and pick her up, to give her money and food. But I also don't want to fool myself. That was just a sop to my conscience and nothing more. It wasn't a real contribution to her life and what she is up against. (*Goes to straighten up the washstand.*) Anyway, what's the point in talking about her? She's most probably curling up in a stormwater drain at this moment . . . that's where she said she'd sleep if she didn't get a lift . . . and I feel better for a good wash.

HELEN. There it is again.

ELSA. Well it's the truth.

HELEN. It was the way you said it.

ELSA. You're imagining things, Miss Helen. Come on, let's talk about something else. It's too soon to get serious. We've got enough time, and reasons, for that later on. What's been happening in the village. Give me the news. Your last letter didn't have much of that in it. (*MISS HELEN starts to fold up the discarded trousers. ELSA stops her.*) I can do that.

HELEN. I just wanted to help.

ELSA. And you can do that by making a nice pot of tea and giving me the village gossip.

(*MISS HELEN brings out cups, saucers and spoons from the kitchen and lays them out on the table. SHE clears the dirty dishes from the table and joins ELSA in the alcove. ELSA has hung up the wet towel, put her dirty cloths into her overnight bag and is now putting moisturizer on her arms, hands and legs.*)

HELEN. I haven't got any gossip. Little Katrina is the only one who visits me anymore and all she wants to talk about these days is her baby. There's also Marius of course, but he never gossips.

ELSA. He still comes snooping around, does he?

HELEN. Don't put it like that, Elsa. He's a very old friend.

ELSA. Good luck to him. I hope the friendship continues. It's just that I wouldn't want him for one. I'm sorry Miss Helen, but I don't trust your old friend and I have a strong feeling Reverend Marius Byleveld feels the same way about me. So let's change the subject. Tell me about Katrina. What has she been up to?

HELEN. She's fine. And so is the baby. As prettily dressed these days as any white baby, thanks to the clothes you sent her. She's been very good to me, Elsa. Never passes my front door without popping in for a little chat. Is always asking about you. I don't know what I would do without her. But I'm afraid Koos has started drinking again. And making all sorts of terrible threats against her and the baby. He still doesn't believe it's his child.

ELSA. Is he beating her?

HELEN. No. The warning you gave him last time seems to have put a stop to that.

ELSA. God it makes me sick! Why doesn't she leave him?

HELEN. And then do what?

ELSA. Find somene else! Someone who will value her as a human being and take care of her and the baby.

HELEN. She can't do that, Elsie. They're married.

ELSA. Oh for God's sake, Helen. There's the Afrikaner in you speaking. There is nothing sacred about a marriage that abuses the woman! I'll have a little talk to her tomorrow. Let's make sure we get a message to her to come around.

(*MISS HELEN puts the dirty dishes in the kitchen. ELSA begins to comb out her hair.*)

HELEN. Don't make things even more difficult for her, Elsa.

ELSA. How much more difficult can "things" be than being married to a drunken bully? She does have some rights, Miss Helen, and I just want to make sure she knows what they are. How old is she now?

HELEN. (*Returning with creamer and sugar bowl.*) Seventeen, I think.

ELSA. Seventeen, at her age I was still at school dreaming about my future and here she is with a baby and bruises. Quick, tell me something else.

HELEN. (*Excited, SHE pulls out a chair and sits.*) Let me see . . . Good gracious me! Of course yes! I have got important news. Brace yourself, Elsa. Old Gertruida has got the whole village up in arms. She's applied for a license to open a Bottle Store.

ELSA. A what?

HELEN. A Bottle Store. With alcoholic beverages.

ELSA. (*Shocked.*) Booze in New Bethesda?

HELEN. (*Taking Elsa seriously.*) Well, if you want to put it that bluntly . . . yes.

ELSA. (*Full of humor.*) Now that is headline material. Good for old Gerty. I always knew she liked her sundowner but I never thought she'd have the spunk to go that far.

HELEN. Don't joke about it Elsie. It's a very serious matter. The village is very upset.

ELSA. Headed no doubt by your old friend the Reverend Marius Byleveld.

HELEN. That's right. I understand that his last sermon was all about the evils of alcohol and how it's ruining the health and lives of our colored folk. Gerty says he's taking unfair advantage of the pulpit and that the coloreds get it anyway from Graaff-Reinet.

ELSA. Then tell her to demand a turn.

HELEN. At what?

ELSA. (*Jumping up on the chaise.*) The pulpit. Tell her to demand her right to get up there and put her case . . . and remind her before she does that the first miracle was water into wine.

HELEN. (*Trying not to laugh.*) You're terrible, Elsie! Old Gerty in the pulpit!

ELSA. And you're an old hypocrite, Helen. You love it when I make fun of the church.

HELEN. (*Struggling to put on her sandals.*) No I don't. I was laughing at Gerty, not the church. And you have no right to make me laugh. It's a very serious matter.

ELSA. (*Helps MISS HELEN buckle her sandals.*) Of course it is! Which is why I want to know who you think is worse . . . The Dominee deciding what is right and wrong for the colored folk, or old Gertruida exploiting their misery.

HELEN. I'm afraid it's even more complicated than that Elsa. Marius is only thinking about what's best for them, but on the other hand Gertruida has offered to donate part of her profits to their school building fund. And what about Koos? Wouldn't it make things even worse for Katrina if he had a local supply?

ELSA. (*Brushes out Miss Helen's hair.*) They are two separate issues, Miss Helen. You don't punish an entire community because one man can't control his drinking. Which raises yet another point: Has anybody bothered to ask the colored people what they think about it all?

HELEN. Are we going to have that argument again?

ELSA. I'm not trying to start an argument. But it does seem to me right and proper that if you're going to make decisions that affect other people, you should find out what those people think.

HELEN. It is the same argument, Elsa. You know they don't do that here.

ELSA. Well it's about time they started. I don't make decisions at school affecting the pupils without giving them a chance to say something. And they're children! We're talking about adult men and women in the year 1974.

HELEN. Those attitudes might be alright in Cape Town, Elsa, but you should know by now that the Valley has got its own way of doing things.

ELSA. (*Braids Miss Helen's hair into a single plait.*) Well it can't cut itself off from the 20th century forever. Honestly, coming here is like stepping into the middle of a Chekhov play. While the rest of the world is hoping the bomb won't drop tomorrow, you people are arguing about who owns the cherry orchard. Your little world is not as safe as you would like to believe, Helen. If you think it's going to left alone to stagnate in the 19th century while the rest of us hold our breath hoping we'll reach the end of the 20th, you're in for one hell of a surprise. And it will start with your colored folk. They're not fools. They also read newspapers, you know. And if you don't believe me try talking about something other than the weather and her baby next time Katrina comes around. You'll be a little surprised at what's going on inside that head of hers. (*Exasperated.*) As for you Helen! Sometimes the contradictions in you make me want to scream. Why do you always stand up and defend this bunch of bigots? Look at the way they've treated you.

HELEN. (*Getting nervous.*) They leave me alone now.

ELSA. That is not what you said in your last letter!

HELEN. (*Nervously pulling at a loose thread on her dress.*) My last letter?

ELSA. Yes. (*Pause. MISS HELEN has tensed.*) Are you saying you don't remember it Helen?

HELEN. No . . . I remember it.

ELSA. And what you said in it?

HELEN. (*Trying to escape.*) Please, little Elsie! Not now. Let's talk about it later. I'm still all flustered with your arriving so unexpectedly. Give me a chance to collect my wits together. And while I'm doing that I'll make that pot of tea you asked for.

(*MISS HELEN exits into the kitchen. ELSA takes stock of the room. Not an idle examination . . . rather a sense that she is trying to see it objectively, trying to understand something . . . She spends a few seconds at the window staring out at the statues in the yard. She sees a cardboard box in a corner and opens . . . handfuls of colored ceramic chips. She also discovers a not very successful attempt to hide an ugly burn mark on the window over the chaise. MISS HELEN returns with tea and biscuits.*)

ELSA. Helen. What happened here?

HELEN. Oh, don't worry about that. I'll get Koos or somebody to clean that up.

ELSA. But what happened?

HELEN. One of the lamps started smoking badly when I was out of the room.

ELSA. And new curtains.

HELEN. Yes. I got tired of the old ones. I found a few Marie biscuits in the pantry. Will you be mother? (*LIGHT is starting to fade in the room. ELSA pours the tea, dividing her attention between that and studying the older woman. MISS HELEN tries to hide her unease.*) Is it my turn now to ask for news?

ELSA. No.

HELEN. Why not?

ELSA. I haven't come up here to talk about myself.

HELEN. That's not fair!

ELSA. It's boring.

HELEN. Not to me. Come on, Elsie, fair is fair. You asked me for the village gossip and I did my best. Now it's your turn.

ELSA. What do you want to know?

HELEN. Everything you would have told me about in your letters if you had kept your promise and written them.

ELSA. (*Pacing around the lounge while sipping her tea.*) Good and bad news?

HELEN. I said everything . . . but try to make the good a little bit more than the bad.

ELSA. Right. The Elsa Barlow Advertiser! Hot off the presses! What do you want to start with? Financial, crime, or sports page?

HELEN. The front page headline.

ELSA. How's this: "Barlow to appear before School Board for possible disciplinary action."

HELEN. Not again!

ELSA. Yep.

HELEN. What was it this time?

ELSA. Wait for the story. "Elsa Barlow, a thirty-one year old English language teacher, is to appear before the Board of Enquiry of the Cape Town School Board. She faces the possibility of strict disciplinary action. The enquiry follows a number of complaints from the parents of pupils in Miss Barlow's Standard Nine class. It is alleged that in April this year Miss Barlow asked the class, as a homework exercise, to write a five hundred word letter to the State President on the subject of racial inequality. Miss Barlow teaches at a colored school."

HELEN. Is that true?

ELSA. Are you doubting the accuracy and veracity of the Advertiser?

HELEN. Elsie! Elsie! Sometimes I think you deliberately look for trouble.

ELSA. All I "deliberately look for," Miss Helen, are opportunities to make those young people in my classroom think for themselves.

HELEN. So what is going to happen?

ELSA. Depends on me. If I appear before them contrite and apologetic . . .   . . . a stern reprimand. But if I behave the way I really feel, I suppose I could lose my job,

HELEN. Do you want my advice?

ELSA. No.

HELEN. Well, I'm going to give it to you all the same. Say you're sorry and that you won't do it again.

ELSA. Both of those are lies, Miss Helen.

HELEN. Only little white ones.

ELSA. God, I'd give anything to be able to walk in there and tell that School Board exactly what I think of them and their educational system. But you're right, there are also the pupils and for as long as I'm in the classroom a little subversion is possible. Rebellion starts, Miss Helen, with just one man, or woman, standing up and saying: "No. Enough!" Albert Camus. French writer.

HELEN. You make me nervous when you talk like that.

ELSA. And you sound just like one of those parents. You know something Helen? I think you're history's first reactionary-revolutionary. You're a double agent!

HELEN. Haven't you got any good news?

ELSA. (*Puts the brush away in her toilet bag.*) Lots. I still don't smoke. I drink very moderately. I try to jog a few miles every morning.

HELEN. You're not saying anything about David.

ELSA. (*Takes a pair of sweat pants out of the overnight*

bag and puts them on under her robe.) Turn to the lonely hearts column. There's a sad little paragraph: "Young woman seeks friendship with young man etc. etc."

HELEN. You're talking in riddles. I was asking you about David.

ELSA. And I'm answering you. I've said nothing about him because there's nothing to say. It's over.

HELEN. You mean . . . you and David?

ELSA. Yes, that is exactly what I mean. It's finished. We don't see each other anymore.

HELEN. I knew there was something wrong from the moment you walked in.

ELSA. (*Puts on a pair of socks.*) If you think this is me with something wrong, you should have been around a couple of months ago. Your little Elsie was in a bad way. You were in line for an unexpected visit a lot earlier than this, Helen.

HELEN. You should have come.

ELSA. I nearly did. But your letters suggested that you weren't having such a good time either. If we'd got together at that point we might have come up with a suicide pact.

HELEN. I don't think so.

ELSA. It's a joke, Miss Helen.

HELEN. Then don't joke about such things. Weren't you going to tell me?

ELSA. (*The breaking point.*) I'm trying to forget it, Helen! (*Sits on the stool in the lounge.*) There's another reason why I didn't come up. It's left me with a profound sense of shame.

HELEN. Of what?

ELSA. Myself. The whole stupid mess!

HELEN. Mess?

ELSA. Yes, mess, have you got a better word to describe a situation so rotten with lies and deceit that the only sense of yourself was one of disgust?

HELEN. And you were so happy when you told me about him on your last visit.

ELSA. God, that was more than just happiness, Miss Helen. It was like discovering the reason for being the person, the woman, I am for the first time in my life. And a little bit scary . . . realizing that another person could do so much to your life, to your sense of yourself. Even before it all went wrong there were a couple of times when I wasn't so sure I liked it.

HELEN. What happened? Was there a row or something?

ELSA. (*Bitter little laugh.*) Row? Oh Helen! Yes, there were plenty of those. But they were incidental. There had to be some sort of noise so we shouted at each other. We also cried. We did everything you're supposed to.

HELEN. All I know about him is what you told me. He seemed such a sensitive and good man, well-read, intelligent. So right for you.

ELSA. He is all of that. (*A moment's hesitation. SHE is not certain about saying something. SHE decides to take the chance.*) There's also something about him I didn't tell you. He's married. He has a devoted, loving wife . . . quite pretty in fact . . . and a child. A little girl. You're shocked.

HELEN. Yes. You should have told me, Elsie. I would have warned you.

ELSA. That's precisely why I didn't. I knew you would, but I was going to prove you wrong. Anyway I didn't need any warnings. Anything you could have said to me I'd said to myself from the very beginning . . . but I was going to prove myself wrong as well. What it all came down to finally is that there were two very different ideas about what was happening, and we discovered it too late. You see, I was in it for keeps, Helen. I knew that we were all going to get hurt, that somehow we would all end up being victims of the situation . . . but I also believed that when the time came to choose I would be the lucky winner, that he would leave his wife and child and go with me. Boy, was I wrong! Ding-dong wrong-wrong . . . tolls Elsa's bell at the close of day!

HELEN. Don't do that.

ELSA. Defense mechanism. It still hurts. I'm getting impatient for the day when I'll be able to laugh at it all. I mustn't make him sound like a complete bastard. He wasn't without a conscience. Far from it. If anything it was too big. The end would have been a lot less messy if he'd known how to just walk away and close the door behind him. When finally the time for that arrived, he sat around in pain and torment . . . crying! . . . God that was awful! . . . waiting for me to tell him to go back to his wife and child. Should have seen him, Helen. He came up with postures of despair that would have made Michelangelo jealous. I know it's all wrong to find another person's pain disgusting but that is eventually what happened. The last time he crucified himself on the sofa in my flat I felt like vomiting. He told me just once too often how much he hated himself for hurting me.

HELEN. Elsie my poor darling. Come here.

ELSA. (*Taut.*) No, I'm all right. (*Pause.*) Do you know what the really big word is, Helen? I had it all wrong. Like most people I suppose I used to think it was "Love." That's a big one alright, and it's quite an event when it comes along. But there's an even bigger one. "Trust." And more dangerous! Because that's when you drop your defenses, lay yourself wide-open and if you've made a mistake you're in big, big trouble. And it hurts like hell. (*Breaking the mood, SHE crosses to Miss Helen.*) Ever heard the story about the father giving his son his first lesson in business? (*MISS HELEN shakes her head.*) I think it's meant to be a joke so remember to laugh. The father puts his little boy high-up on something or other and says to him: "Jump. Don't worry. I'll catch you." The child is nervous of course but Daddy keeps reassuring him: "I'll catch you." Eventually the little boy works up enough courage and does jump and of course his father doesn't make a move to catch him. When the child has stopped crying . . . because he hurt himself . . . the father says: "Your first lesson in business, my son. Don't trust anybody." (*Pause.*) If you tell it with a Jewish accent it's even funnier.

(*Sits at the table with MISS HELEN.*)

HELEN. I don't think it's funny.

ELSA. I think it's ugly. That little boy is going to think twice about jumping again and at this moment the same goes for Elsa Barlow.

HELEN. Don't speak too soon, Elsie. Life has surprised me once or twice.

ELSA. I'm talking about "Trust," Miss Helen. I can see myself loving somebody again . . . not all that interested in it right at the moment, but there's an even chance that it will happen again. Doesn't seem as if we've got much choice in the matter. But trusting?

HELEN. You can have the one without the other?

ELSA. Oh yes. That much I've learnt. I went on loving David long after I realized I couldn't trust him anymore. That is why life is still just a bit complicated at the moment. A little of that love is still hanging around.

HELEN. I've never really thought about it.

ELSA. Neither had I. It needs a betrayal to get you going.

HELEN. Then I suppose I've been lucky. I never had any important trusts to betray . . . until I met you. My marriage might have looked like that but it was habit that kept Stefanus and me together. I was never really . . . open? . . . to him. Was that the phrase you used?

ELSA. Wide-open.

HELEN. That's it! It's a good one. I was never "wide-open" to anybody. But with you all of that changed. So it's as simple as that. Trust. I've always tried to understand what made you, and being with you, so different from anything else in my life. But of course, that's it. I trust you. That's why my little girl can come out and play. All the doors are wide-open!

ELSA. (*Breaking the mood.*) So there, Miss Helen. You asked for the news . . .

HELEN. I almost wish I hadn't. Oh, it's getting dark.

(*LIGHT has now faded. MISS HELEN puts the moon candle on the table and LIGHTS it. The room floats-up gently out of the gloom, the mirrors and glitter on the walls reflecting the candlelight. MISS HELEN goes into the back room and puts on her cardigan. ELSA picks up the moon candle and walks around the room with it and we see something of the magic to come.*)

ELSA. (*Full of joy.*) Still works, Miss Helen. Driving up here in the car I was wondering if the novelty would have worn-off a little. But here it is again. You're a little wizard you know. You make magic with your mirrors and glitter. (*LIGHTS the candle on the washstand.*) "Never light a candle carelessly, and be sure you know what you're doing when you blow one out." Remember saying that?

HELEN. To myself, yes. Many times.

ELSA. And to me . . . after you had stopped laughing at the expression on my face when you lit them for the first time. "Light is a miracle, Miss Barlow, which even the most ordinary human being can make happen." We had just had our first pot of tea together. Maybe I do take it all just a little bit for granted now. But that first time . . . (*LIGHTS a candle on the shaker table.*) I wish I could make you realize what it's like to be walking down a dusty, deserted little street in a Godforsaken village in the middle of the Karoo, bored to death by heat and the flies and the silence, and then to be stopped in your tracks . . . and I mean stopped! (*LIGHTS the candle on the oriental table.*) . . . by all of that out there. And then, having barely recovered from that, to come inside and find this! (*Puts the moon candle down on the table.*) Believe me, Helen, when I saw your "Mecca" for the first time, I just stood there and gaped. (*Looking out to the yard with Miss Helen's statues.*) "What in God's name am I looking at? Camels and pyramids? Not three, but dozens of Wise Men? Owls with old motorcar headlights for eyes? Peacocks with more color and glitter than the real birds? Heat stroke? Am I hallucinating?" And then you! Standing next to a Mosque made out of beer bottles and staring back at me like one of your owls! (*A good laugh at the memory.*) She's mad. No question about it. Everything they've told me about her is absolutely true. A genuine Karoo nutcase. (*Walking carefully around Miss Helen in a mock attitude of wary suspicious examination.*) Doesn't look dangerous though. Wait . . . she's smiling! Be careful, Barlow! Could be a trick. They didn't say she was violent though. Just mad. Mad as a hatter. Go on. Take a chance. Say Hello and see what happens. "Hello!" (*Both WOMEN laugh.*)

HELEN. Hello! You're exaggerating. It wasn't like that at all.

ELSA. Yes it was.

HELEN. And I'm saying it wasn't. To start with, it wasn't the Mosque. I was repairing a mermaid.

ELSA. I forgot the mermaids!

HELEN. (*Serenely certain.*) And I was the one who spoke first. I asked you to point out the directions to Mecca, you made a mistake and so I corrected you. Then I invited you into the yard, showed you around after which we came in here for that pot of tea.

ELSA. That is precisely what I mean! Who would ever believe it? That you found yourself being asked to point out the direction to Mecca . . . not London, or New York or Paris, but Mecca . . . in the middle of the Karoo by a little lady no bigger than a bird, surrounded by camels and owls . . . and mermaids! . . . made of cement? Who in their right mind is going to believe that? And then this . . . (*The room.*) . . . your little miracle of light and color. (*MISS HELEN is smiling with suppressed pride and pleasure.*) You were proud of yourself, weren't you? Come on, admit it. (*Sits at the table.*)

HELEN. (*Trying hard to contain her emotion.*) Yes, I admit I was a little proud.

ELSA. Miss Helen? Just a little?

HELEN. (*Can't hold back any longer.*) Alright then . . . No! Not just a little. I was prouder of myself that day than I had ever been in my life. Nobody before you, or since, had done that to me. I've got a silly little confession to make about that first meeting. When we came inside and were sitting in here talking and drinking tea and the light started to fade and it became time to light a candle . . . I suddenly realized I was beginning to feel shy, more shy than I had ever been with Stefanus on my wedding night. It got so bad I was half-wishing you would stand up and say it was time to go! You see, when I lit the candles you were finally going to see all of me. I don't mean my face, or the clothes I was wearing . . . you had already seen all of that out in the yard . . . But the real me, because that is what this room is . . . and I so desperately, wanted you to like what you saw. By the time we met I had got used to the rude eyes staring at me and my work, dismissing both of them as ugly. I'd lived with those eyes for fifteen years and they didn't bother me anymore. Yours were different. In just the short time we had been together I had ended up feeling . . . No. More than that . . . I *knew* I could trust them. There's our big word again, Elsie! I was so nervous I didn't know what we were talking about anymore while I sat here trying to find enough courage to get a box of matches and light the candles. But eventually I did and you . . . you looked around the room and laughed with delight! You liked what you saw! This is the best of me, Elsa. This is what I really am. Nothing, not even my name or my face, is me as much as those Wise Men and their camels travelling to the East, or the light and glitter in this room. The mermaids, the wise old owls, the gorgeous peacocks . . . all of them are *me.* And I had delighted you! Dear God. If you only knew what you did for my life that day. How much courage, how much faith in it you gave me. Because all those years of being laughed at and called a mad old woman had taken their toll, Elsie. When you walked into my life that afternoon I hadn't been able to work or make anything for nearly a year . . . and I was beginning to think I wouldn't ever again . . . that I had reached the end. You revived my life. I didn't sleep that night after you left. My Mecca was a long way from being finished! All the things I still had to do, all the statues I still had to make came crowding in on me when I went to bed. I thought my head was going to burst! I've never been so impatient with darkness all my life. I just sat up in bed all night waiting for the dawn to come so that I could start working again, and then just go on working and working.

ELSA. And you certainly did that, Miss Helen. On my next visit you proudly introduced me to a very stern Buddha, remember. The cement was still wet.

HELEN. (*Runs over to the window and looks out at the yard.*) That's quite right. That was my next one.

ELSA. Then came the Easter Island head . . . the one with the top-knot.

HELEN. Correct.

ELSA. And you still haven't explained to me what it's doing in Mecca . . . and for that matter wise old owls and mermaids as well.

HELEN. My Mecca has got its own logic, Elsa. Even I don't properly understand it.

ELSA. (*Joining Miss Helen.*) And then my favorite! That strange creature . . . half cock, half man . . . on the point of dropping his trousers. Really, Helen!

HELEN. That one is pure imagination. I don't know where he comes from. And I've told you before Elsie he's not dropping his trousers, he's pulling them up.

ELSA. (*Pointing to the statue in question.*) And I remain unconvinced. Take another good look at the expression on his face. That's anticipation, not satisfaction. (*THEY laugh. ELSA gives Miss Helen a hug.*) Any surprises this time? (*Pause.*)

HELEN. This time?

ELSA. Yes.

HELEN. (*Distracted.*) No. No surprises this time.

ELSA. Works in progress?

HELEN. (*Fusses with the teapot.*) Not at the moment. I haven't managed to get started on anything since you were last here.

ELSA. What happened to that splendid idea for a moon-mosaic against the back wall? You were going to use those ceramic chips I brought you.

HELEN. (*Pointing to the box of chips.*) They're safe. Look, over there.

ELSA. Yes, I saw them . . . in exactly the same spot I left them three months ago. It sounded such a wonderful idea, Helen. You were so excited when you told me about it.

HELEN. (*Defensively.*) And I still am. I've still got it.

ELSA. So what are you waiting for, roll up your sleeves and get on with it.

HELEN. (*The breaking point.*) It's not as simple as that, Elsa. That's just the trouble. It's still only just an *idea* I'm *thinking* about. I can't see it clearly enough yet to start work on it. I've told you before Elsie I have to *see* them very clearly first . . . they've got to come to me inside like pictures . . . and if they don't, well all I can do is wait . . . and hope that they will. I wish I knew how to make it happen, but I don't. I don't know where the pictures come from. I can't force myself to see something that isn't there. I've tried to do that once or twice in the past when I was desperate but the work always ended up a shapeless, lifeless mess. If they don't come all I can do is wait . . . which is what I'm doing now.

(*HELEN is revealing a lot of inner agitation.*)

ELSA. (*Carefully.*) Go on, Helen. I'm listening.

HELEN. I try to be patient with myself, but it's hard. There isn't all that much time left . . . and then my eyes . . . and my hands . . . they're not what they used to be. But the worst thing of all is . . . suppose I'm waiting for nothing! That there aren't going to be any more pictures inside ever again . . . That this time I *have* reached the end. Do you understand what I am saying, Elsie?

ELSA. I think I do. (*SHE speaks quietly. It is not going to be easy.*) Come and sit down here with me, Helen. (*MISS HELEN sits down near her, but apprehensively.*) It's time to talk about your last letter, Helen.

HELEN. Must we do that now? Can't it wait?

ELSA. No.

HELEN. Please.

ELSA. Sorry Helen, but we've only got tonight.

HELEN. Then don't spoil it!

ELSA. Helen . . . that letter is the reason for my being here. You do realize that, don't you?

HELEN. Yes. I guessed that was the reason for your visit. But you must make allowances, little Elsie. I wasn't feeling very well when I wrote it.

ELSA. That much is obvious.

HELEN. But I've cheered up ever so much since then. Truly. And now with your visit and everything . . . I just know everything is going to be alright again. I was very depressed you see. I wrote it in a bad depression. But I regretted posting it the moment after I had dropped it into the letter box. I even thought about asking the Postmaster if I could have it back.

ELSA. Why didn't you? (*Pause.*) Or send me a telegram. "Ignore last letter. Feeling much better." Six words. That would have done it.

HELEN. I never thought of that.

ELSA. We're wasting precious time. You wrote it, posted it and I received it.

HELEN. So can't we please just forget it?

ELSA. (*Disbelief.*) Miss Helen? Do you remember what you said in it?

HELEN. Vaguely.

ELSA. That's not good enough.

(*Goes to the bedroom alcove where she fetches the letter from her briefcase.*)

HELEN. What are you going to do?

ELSA. Read it.

HELEN. No! I don't want to hear it.

ELSA. You already have, Miss Helen. You wrote it.

HELEN. But I don't want to talk about it.

ELSA. Yes, you are.

HELEN. Don't bully me, Elsa! You know I don't know how to fight back. Please . . . not tonight. Can't we . . .

ELSA. No we can't. For God's sake, Helen! We've only got tonight and maybe a little bit of tomorrow to talk.

HELEN. But you mustn't take it seriously.

ELSA. (*Beginning to lose her patience.*) Too late, Helen. I already have. I've driven eight hundred miles without break because of this. And don't lie to me. You meant every word of it. (*Pause. In a gentler tone.*) I'm not trying to punish you for having written it. I've come because I want to try and help. (*Sits down at the table, pulls the candle closer and reads. SHE struggles a little bit to decipher words, the handwriting is obviously bad.*) "My very own and dearest little Elsie, Have you finally also deserted me? This is my fourth letter to you and still no reply. Have I done something wrong? This must surely be the darkest night of my soul. I thought I had lived through that fifteen years ago, but I was wrong. This is worse. Infinitely worse. I had nothing to lose that night. Nothing in my life was precious or worth holding onto. Now there is so much and I am losing it all . . . you, the house, my work, my Mecca. I can't fight them alone, little Elsie. I need you. Don't you care about me anymore? It is only through your eyes that I now see my Mecca. I need you, Elsie. My eyesight is so bad that I can barely see the words I am writing. And my hands can hardly hold the pen. Help me, little Elsie. Everything is ending and I am alone in the dark. There is no light left. I would rather do away with myself than carry on like this. Your ever loving and anguished, Helen." (*Carefully folds up the letter and puts it back in the envelope.*) What's all that about losing your house? Who's trying to get you out?

HELEN. I exaggerated in my letter. They're not really being nasty about it.

ELSA. Who?

HELEN. The Church Council. They say it's for my own good . . . and I do understand what they mean, it's just that . . .

ELSA. Slowly, Miss Helen, slowly. I still don't know what you're talking about. Start from the beginning. What has the Church Council got to do with you and the house? I thought it was yours?

HELEN. It is.

ELSA. So?

HELEN. It's not the house, Elsa. It's me . . . they discussed me . . . my situation . . . at one of their meetings.

ELSA. (*Disbelief and anger.*) They what?

HELEN. That's how Marius put it. He . . . he said they were worried about me living here alone.

ELSA. *They* are worried about *you?*

HELEN. Yes. It's my health they are worried about.

ELSA. (*Shaking her head.*) When it comes to hypocrisy . . . and blatant hypocrisy at that . . . you Afrikaners are in a class by yourself. So tell me, did they also discuss Gertruida's situation? And what about Mrs. van Heerden down at the other end of the village? They're about the same age as you and they also live alone.

HELEN. That's what I said. But Marius said it's different with them.

ELSA. In what way?

HELEN. Well you see because of my hands and everything, they don't think I can look after myself so well anymore.

ELSA. Are they right?

HELEN. No! I'm quite capable of looking after myself.

ELSA. And where are you supposed to go if you leave the village? A niece, four times removed, in Durban, who you've only seen a couple of times in your life? (*MISS HELEN takes the red box out of the sideboard, opens it and hands a form to Elsa. Reading.*) Sonskyn Tehuis Vir Ons Oues Van Dae. "Sunshine Home for Our Aged." I see. So it's like that, is it? That's the lovely old house on the left when you come into Graaff-Reinet . . . next to the church. In fact it's run by the church, isn't it?

HELEN. Yes.

ELSA. (*Crooked humor. We see the edge of Elsa's wit.*) That figures. It's got a beautiful garden, Miss Helen. Whenever I drive past on my way up here there's always a few old folk in their "twilight years" sitting around enjoying the sunshine. It's well named. It all looks very restful. So that's what they want to do with you. This is not your handwriting.

HELEN. No. Marius filled it in for me.

ELSA. Very considerate of him.

HELEN. He's coming to fetch it tonight.

ELSA. For an old friend he sounds a little over-eager to have you on your way, Miss Helen.

HELEN. It's just that they've got a vacancy at the moment. They're usually completely full. There's a long waiting list. But I haven't signed it yet!

(*ELSA studies Miss Helen in silence for a few moments.*)

ELSA. How bad are your hands? Be honest with me.

HELEN. (*Hiding her hands in her lap.*) They're not *that* bad. I exaggerated in my letter.

ELSA. You could still work with them if you wanted to?

HELEN. Yes.

ELSA. Is there anything you can't do?

HELEN. I can do anything I want to, Elsie . . . if I make the effort.

ELSA. Let me see them.

HELEN. Please don't. I'm ashamed of them.

ELSA. Come on. (*MISS HELEN holds out her hands. ELSA examines them.*) And these scabs?

HELEN. They're nothing. A little accident at the stove. I was making prickly-pear syrup for you.

ELSA. There seems to have been a lot of little accidents lately. Better be more careful.

HELEN. I will. I definitely will.

ELSA. Pain?

HELEN. Just a little.

ELSA. Alright, so what are you going to do when he comes around? (*MISS HELEN doesn't answer. She clutches the box and puts it back in the sideboard. ELSA is beginning to lose patience.*) Come on Helen! If I hadn't

turned up tonight what were you going to say to Dominee Marius Byleveld?

HELEN. I was going to ask him to give me a little more
time to think about it.

ELSA. You were going to *ask* him for it, not *tell* him
you *wanted* it. And *do* you need more time to think
about it? I thought you knew what you wanted?

HELEN. Of course I do.

ELSA. (*Firmly.*) Then tell me again. And say it clearly.
I need to hear it.

HELEN. You know I can't leave here, Elsa!

ELSA. For a moment I wasn't so sure. So then what's
the problem? When he comes around tonight hand this
back to him . . . unsigned . . . and say no. Thank
him for his trouble but tell him you are prefectly happy
where you are and quite capable of looking after yourself. (*Holds out the form to Miss Helen. MISS HELEN
hesitates. A sense of increasing emotional confusion and
uncertainty.*) Helen, you have just said that is what you
want.

HELEN. I know. It's just that Marius is such a persua-
sive talker.

ELSA. Then talk back!

HELEN. I'm not very good at that. Won't you help me,
little Elsie . . . please! . . . and speak to him as well.
You are so much better at arguing than me.

ELSA. No, I won't! And for God's sake stop behaving
like a naughty child who's been summoned to the principal's office. I'm sorry, but the more I hear about your
Marius the worse it gets. If you want my advice you'll
keep the two of us well away from each other. I *won't*
argue with him on your behalf because there is nothing
to argue about. This is not his house and it most certainly
is not his life that is being discussed at Church Council

meetings. Who the hell do they think they are? Sitting around a table deciding what is going to happen to you!

HELEN. Marius did say that they were trying to think of what was best for me.

ELSA. No, they're not! God knows what they're thinking about but it's certainly not that. Dumping you with a lot of old people who've hung-on for too long and nobody wants around anymore? You're still living your life Helen, not drooling it away. The only legal way they can get you out of this house is by having you certified. (*Awkward silence.*) We all know you're as mad as a hatter, but it's not quite that bad. (*Another pause.*) One little question though Miss Helen. You haven't been going around talking about "doing away with yourself" to anyone have you?

HELEN. I told you Katrina is the only one who visits me anymore.

ELSA. And Marius. Don't forget him. Anyway it doesn't matter who it is. All it needs is one person to be able to stand-up and testify that they heard you say it.

HELEN. Well I haven't. (*Nervously fidgeting with the candle and matches on the shaker table.*)

ELSA. Because it would make life a lot easier for them if they ever did try to do something. So no more of that. Alright? Did you hear me, Helen?

HELEN. Yes, I heard you.

ELSA. And while you're about it, add me to your list. I don't want to hear, or read anymore about it either.

HELEN. I heard you Elsie! Why do you keep on about it?

ELSA. Because talk like that could be grounds for forcibly committing someone to a "Sunshine Home for Our Aged!" I'm sorry, Helen, but what do you expect me to do? Pretend you never said it? Is that what you would have done if the situations had been reversed? If in the middle of my mess I had threatened to do that? God knows I came near to feeling like it a couple of times. I had a small taste of how bloody pointless everything can seem to be. But if I can hang on, then you most certainly don't throw in the towel . . . not after all the rounds you've already won against them. So when the Dominee comes around you're going to put on a brave front. (*Puts her arm around Miss Helen's shoulder and leads her back gently to her chair at the table.*) But first let's get him and his stupid idea about an old age home right out of your life. Because you're going to say "No," remember. Be as polite and civil as you like . . . we'll offer him tea and biscuits and discuss the weather and the evils of alcohol . . . but when the time comes you're going to thank him for all his trouble and consideration and then hand this back to him with a firm "No thank you." (*Another idea.*) And just to make quite sure he gets the message you can also mention your trip into Graaff-Reinet next week to see a doctor and an optician.

HELEN. What do you mean?

ELSA. Exactly what I said. Appointments with a doctor and an optician. (*Puts the letter back in her briefcase.*)

HELEN. But I haven't got any.

ELSA. You will on Monday. Before I leave tomorrow I'm going to ask Gertruida to take you into Graaff-Reinet next week. And this time you're going to go. There must be something they can do about your hands, even if it's just to ease the pain. And a little "regmaker" for your depressions. (*MISS HELEN wants to say something.*) No arguments! And to hell with your vanity as well. We all know you think you're the prettiest thing in the village but if you need glasses you're going to wear them. I'll make the appointments myself and phone through after you've been in to find out what the verdict is. I'm not trying to be funny, Helen. You've got to prove to the village that you are quite capable of looking after yourself. It's the only way to shut them up.

HELEN. You're going too fast for me, Elsa. You're not allowing me to say anything.

ELSA. (*Sitting at the table.*) That's quite right. How many times in the past haven't we sat down and tried to talk about all of this? and everytime the same story: "I'll think about it Elsa." Your thinking has got us nowhere, Helen. This time you're just going to agree . . . and that includes letting Katrina come in a couple of times each week to do the house.

HELEN. There's nothing for her to do. I can manage by myself.

ELSA. No you can't.

(*Runs her finger over a piece of furniture and holds it up for MISS HELEN to see the dust.*)

HELEN. Everything would have been spotless if I had known you were coming.

ELSA. It's got to be spotless all the time! To hell with my visit and holidays. I don't live here. You do. It's your life I am concerned with, Helen. And I'm also not blind you know. I saw you struggling with that large kettle. Yes, let's talk about that. When did you last boil up enough water for a decent bath? Come on, Helen. Can't you remember? Some time ago, right? Is that because of personal neglect, that you've stopped caring about yourself, or that you weren't able to? Answer me.

HELEN. I can't listen to you anymore, Elsa. (*Makes a move to leave the room.*)

ELSA. Don't do that to me, Helen! If you leave this

room I'm getting into my car and driving back to Cape Town. You wrote that letter. I haven't made it up. All I'm trying to do is deal with it.

HELEN. No you're not.

ELSA. Then I give up. What in God's name have we been talking about?

HELEN. A pair of spectacles and medicine for my arthritis and Katrina dusting the house . . .

ELSA. (*Confronts Miss Helen face on.*) Do you want me to read it again?

HELEN. (*Ignoring the interuption.*) You're treating that letter like a shopping list. That isn't what I was writing about.

ELSA. Then what were you?

HELEN. Darkness, Elsa! Yes. Darkness! (*SHE speaks with an emotional intensity and authority which forces Elsa to listen in silence.*) The Darkness that nearly smothered my life in here one night fifteen years ago. The same Darkness that used to come pouring down the chimney and into the room at night when I was a little girl and frighten me. If you still don't know what I'm talking about, blow out the candle! But those were easy Darknesses to deal with. The one I'm talking about is much worse. It's inside me Elsa . . . it's got inside me at last and I can't light candles there. (*Pause. MISS HELEN wanders from candle to candle, reaching out to them. SHE eventually settles on the edge of the chaise and picks up the candle in a glass-faceted holder from the oriental table.*) I never knew that could happen. I thought I was safe. I had grown up and I had all the candles I wanted. That is all that little girl could think about when she lay there in bed, trying to make her prayers last as long as she could because she was terrified of the moment when her mother would bend down and kiss her and take away the candle. One day she would have her very own! That was the promise. That one day when I was big enough, she would leave one at my bedside for me to light as often as I wanted. That's all that "getting big" ever meant to me. . . . my very own candle at my bedside. Such brave little lights! And they taught the little girl how to be that. When she saw one burning in the middle of the night she knew what courage was. (*Puts down the candle on the table.*) All my life they have helped me to find courage . . . until now. (*Turns towards Elsa.*) I'm frightened, Elsie, more frightened than that little girl ever was. There's no "getting big" left to wait for, no prayers to say until that happens . . . and the candles don't help anymore. That is what I was trying to tell you. I'm frightened. And Marius can see it. He's no fool. He knows that his moment has finally come.

ELSA. What moment?

HELEN. He's been waiting a long time for me to reach the end of my Mecca. I thought I had cheated him out of it, that that moment would never come. (*Looking out at her yard.*) All those years when I was working away, when it was slowly taking shape, he was there as well . . . standing in the distance, watching and waiting. I used to peep at him through the curtains. He'd come walking past, then stop, stand there at the gate with his hands behind his back and stare at my Wise Men. And even though he never showed anything, I knew he didn't like what he saw. I used to sing while I was working. He heard me one day and came up and asked: "Are you really that happy, Helen?" I laughed. Not at *him*, believe me not at him, but because I had a secret he would never understand. (*Pause.*) It's his turn to laugh now. But he won't of course. He's not that sort of man.

He'll be very gentle again . . . pull the curtains and close the shutters the way he did that night fifteen years ago . . . because nobody must stare in at a house where there's been a death. If my Mecca is finished, Elsa, then so is my life.

(*ELSA is overwhelmed by a sense of helplessness and defeat. She sits at the table.*)

ELSA. I think I've had it. It's too much for one day. That woman on the road and now you. I really don't know how to handle it. In fact, at this moment, I don't think I know anything. I don't know what it means to be walking eighty miles to Cradock with your baby on your back. I don't know if your Mecca is finished or not. And all I know about Darkness is that that is when you put on the light. Jesus! I wouldn't mind somebody coming along and telling me what it does all mean. So where does that leave us, Miss Helen? I'm lost. What are you going to do when he comes? (*No answer.*) Ask him . . . please! . . . for more time? One thing I can tell you right now, there's no point to that. If you don't say "No" tonight, you never will, in which case you might as well sign that form and get it over and done with. (*A cruel, relentless tone in her voice.*) There's no point in talking about anything until that's settled. So you better think about it Helen. While you do that I'll see what I can organize for supper.

(*SHE exits into the kitchen with the moon candle. MISS HELEN leaves the window and sits at the table. A MAN'S VOICE off . . . "Anybody at home?" MARIUS appears in the doorway.*)

MARIUS. Miss Helen! Alone in the dark? I thought nobody was home. (*Elsa appears from the kitchen holding the moon candle.*) Ah! . . . Miss Barlow.

CURTAIN

ACT II

SCENE: (The same a few minutes later.

AT RISE: *ELSA has hung up the robe and put on a sweater. SHE enters from the kitchen with the tray and begins to clear the dirty dishes from the table. MARIUS and MISS HELEN are now standing around the table . . . the center of attraction being a basket of vegetables which MARIUS brought with him. He is about the same age as MISS HELEN. Neatly dressed in a dark two piece suit, white shirt, tie and a dark wool vest. HE speaks with simple sincerity and charm.)*

MARIUS. (*Holding up a potato.*) Feast your eyes on that, Miss Barlow! A genuine Sneeuberg potato! A pinch of salt and you've got a meal, and if you want to be extravagant, add a little butter and you have indeed got a feast. We had a farmer from the Gamtoos Valley up here last week, trying to sell potatoes to us! Can you believe it? Did you see him, Helen? He had his lorry parked in front of the Post Office. What's the English expression, Miss Barlow? "Coals to . . . " Where?

ELSA. Coals to Newcastle.

MARIUS. That's it! Well in this case it was very near to being an insult as well. We pride ourselves in these parts on knowing what a potato really is. And here you have it. Art Appel The Apple of the Earth, as we Afrikaners say. (*ELSA exits with the tray of dishes.*) But I don't imagine that poor man will come again. Shame! I ended up feeling very sorry for him. "Don't you people like potatoes?" he asked me. What could I say? I didn't have the heart to tell him he'd wasted his time driving all this distance, that *nobody* comes to the Sneeuberg to sell potatoes! And then to make me feel really bad he insisted on giving me a small sack of them before he drove off. I don't think he sold enough to cover the cost of his petrol back home. (*ELSA returns to retrieve the teapot. MARIUS is involved with the contents of the basket.*) I also brought you some beets and tomatoes. The beets have passed their best now but if you pickle and bottle them they'll be more than alright. Have you ever treated our young friend to a taste of that, Miss Helen? (*To Elsa.*) It's one of our local specialities Miss Barlow. (*ELSA goes back into the kitchen.*) One thing I can assure you ladies is that these vegetables are as fresh as you are ever likely to get. I dug them out myself this afternoon.

HELEN. It's very kind of you, Marius, but you really shouldn't have bothered.

(*ELSA, back in the bedroom alcove, takes her sneakers out of her overnight bag and sits down on the lounge stool to put them on.*)

MARIUS. It wasn't any bother at all. I've got more than enough for myself stored away in the pantry. Would have been a sin to leave them to rot in the ground when somebody else could use them. And at our age we need fresh vegetables, Helen. (*Wagging a finger at her.*) Marie biscuits and tea is not a balanced diet. (*Looks out to the yard, with potato in hand.*) In the old days Miss Helen used to have a very fine vegetable garden of her own out there. But as you can see the humble potato has been crowded out by other things. (*To Elsa.*) I don't think there's enough room left out there now to grow a radish. (*Back to the basket.*) Yes, the Good Lord was very good to us this past year. I don't really know that we deserve it but our rains came just when we needed them. Not too much or too little. Believe me, young lady, we are well experienced in both those possibilities. Not so, Helen?

ELSA. The Karoo looked very dry and desolate to me as I drove through it this afternoon.

MARIUS. (*Trying to make polite conversation.*) Dry it certainly is, but not desolate. It might appear that to a townsman's eye . . . as indeed it did to mine when I first came here! . . . but that is because we are already deep into our autumn. It will be some months before we see rain again.

ELSA. I've never thought of this world as having seasons . . . certainly not the soft ones. To me it has always been a landscape of extremes, too hot or too cold, too dry or else Miss Helen is writing to me about floods that have cut-off the village from the outside world. It reminds me of something I once read where the desert was described as "God without Mankind."

MARIUS. What an interesting thought. "God without Mankind." I can't decide whether that's Catholic or Protestant. Would you know?

ELSA. (*Shaking her head.*) No.

MARIUS. Who wrote it?

ELSA. A French writer. Balzac.

MARIUS. Balzac!

ELSA. It sums up the way I feel about the Karoo. The Almighty hasn't exactly made mankind overwelcome here has he? In fact it almost looks as if he resented our presence. Sorry, Dominee, I don't mean to be blasphemous or ungenerous to your world, its just that I'm used to a gentler one.

MARIUS. (*Crosses to Elsa.*) You judge it too harshly, Miss Barlow. It has got its gentle moments and moods as well . . . all the more precious because there are so few of them. We can't afford to take them for granted. As you can see, it feeds us. Can any man or woman ask for more than that from the little bit of earth they live on? (*Returns to his basket.*)

ELSA. Do you think your colored folk feel the same way about things?

MARIUS. (*Caught off guard.*) Why should it be any different for them?

ELSA. I was just wondering whether they had as many reasons to be as contented as you?

MARIUS. I was talking about simple gratitude, Miss Barlow. Wouldn't you say contentment was a more complicated state of mind? One that can very easily be disturbed! But grateful? . . . Yes? Our colored folk also have every reason to be. Ask them. Ask little Katrina who visits Miss Helen so faithfully, whether she and her baby have ever wanted for food . . . even when Koos has spent all his wages on liquor. There are no hungry people — white or colored — in this village, Miss Barlow. Those of us who are more fortunate than others are well aware of the responsibilities that go with that good fortune. But I don't want to get into an argument. It is my world . . . and Helen's! . . . and we mustn't expect an outsider to love and understand it as we do.

ELSA. (*Picking up the basket.*) I'll put these away for you, Miss Helen.

MARIUS. Don't bother to unpack them now. I'll collect the basket tomorrow after church. (*Calling after her as she goes into the kitchen.*) And there's also no need to wash them, Miss Barlow. I've already done that. Just put them straight into the pot. I've got a feeling that given half a chance your young friend and myself *could* very easily find ourselves in an argument. I think Miss Barlow gets a little impatient with our old-fashioned ways and attitudes. But it's too late for us to change now. Right, Helen?

HELEN. Elsa and I have already had those arguments, Marius.

MARIUS. I hope you put up a good defense on our behalf.

HELEN. I tried my best.

MARIUS. And yet the two of you still remain good friends.

HELEN. Oh yes!

MARIUS. And so it should be. A true friendship should be able to accommodate a difference of opinion. You didn't mention anything about her coming up for a visit last time we talked.

HELEN. Because I didn't know. It's an unexpected visit.

MARIUS. Will she be staying long?

HELEN. Just tonight. She goes back tomorrow.

MARIUS. Good heavens! All this way for only one night. I hope nothing is wrong.

HELEN. No! She just decided on the spur of the moment to visit me. But she's got to go back because they're very busy at school. They're right in the middle of exams.

MARIUS. I see. Helen, may I sit down for a moment?

HELEN. Of course, Marius. Forgive me, I'm forgetting my manners.

MARIUS. (*Hangs up hat and scarf in the hallway and then joins Helen at the table.*) I won't stay long. I must put down a few thoughts for tomorrow's sermon. And thanks to you I know what I want to say.

HELEN. Me?

MARIUS. Yes, you. (*Teasing her.*) You are responsible . . .

HELEN. Oh dear!

MARIUS. (*A little laugh.*) Relax, Helen. I only said thanks to you because it came to me this afternoon while I was digging up your vegetables. I spent a lot of time while I was out in the garden doing that, just leaning on my spade. My back is giving me a bit of trouble again and to tell you the truth, I also felt lazy. I wasn't thinking about anything in particular . . . just looking, you know, the way an old man does, looking around, recognizing once again and saying the names. Spitskop in the distance! Aasvoëlkrans down at the other end of the valley. The poplars with their autumn foliage standing around as yellow and bright as that candle flame! And a lot of remembering. As you know, Helen, I had deep and very painful wounds in my soul when I first came here. Wounds I thought would never heal. This was going to be where I finally escaped from life, turned my back on it and justified what was left of my existence by ministering to you people's simple needs. I was very wrong. I didn't escape from life here, I discovered it, what it really means, the fullness and goodness of it. It's a deep and lasting regret that Aletta wasn't alive to share that discovery with me. Anyway, all of this was going on in my head when I realized I was hearing a small little voice, and the small little voice was saying "thank you." With every spade-full of earth that I turned, when I went down on my knees to lift the potatoes out of the soil, there it was: Thank you. It was mine! I was muttering away to myself the way we old folks are inclined to do when nobody is around. It was me saying "thank you." That is what I want to do tomorrow, Helen. Give thanks, but in a way that I've never done before. I know I've stood there in the pulpit many times telling all of you to do exactly that, but oh dear me! the cleverness and conceit in the soul of

Marius Byleveld when he was doing that. I had an actor's vanity up there, Helen. I'm not saying I was a total hypocrite, but believe me in those thanksgivings I was listening to my Dominee's voice and its hoped-for eloquence every bit as much as to the true little voice inside my heart . . . the voice I heard so clearly this afternoon. That's the voice that must speak tomorrow! And to do that I must find words as simple as the sky I was standing under or the earth I was turning over with my spade. They have got no vanities or conceits. They are just "there." And if the Almighty takes pity on us, the one gives us rain so that the other can in turn . . . give us this day our daily potato. (*A smile at this gentle little joke.*) Am I making any sense, Helen? Answer me truthfully.

HELEN. Yes, you are Marius. And if all you do tomorrow is say what you have just said to me, it will be very moving and beautiful.

MARIUS. (*Sincerely.*) Truly, Helen? Do you really mean that?

HELEN. Every word of it.

MARIUS. Then I will try. (*Rests his hand on HELEN's. THEY both withdraw. A pause.*) My twentieth anniversary comes up next month. Yes, that is how long I've been here. Twenty-one years ago, May the sixteenth, the Good Lord called my Aletta to his side and just over a year later, June the eleventh, I gave my first sermon in New Bethesda. (*A little laugh at the memory.*) What an occasion that was! I don't know if I showed it, Helen, but let me confess now that I was more than just a little nervous when I went up into the pulpit and looked down at the stern and formidable array of faces. A very different proposition to the town and city congregations I had been preaching to up until then. When Miss de Klerk played the first bars of the hymn at the end of it, I heaved a very deep sigh of relief. None of you had fallen asleep! (*HELEN is shaking her head.*) What's the matter, Helen?

HELEN. Young Miss de Klerk came later. Mrs. Retief was still our organist when you gave your first service.

MARIUS. Are you sure?

HELEN. Yes. Mrs. Retief also played at the reception we gave you afterwards in Mr. van Heerden's house. She played the piano and Sterling Retief sang.

MARIUS. You know something, I do believe you're right! Good heavens, Helen, your memory is better than mine.

HELEN. And you had no cause to be nervous, Marius. You were very impressive.

MARIUS. (*A small pause as HE remembers something else.*) Yes, of course. You were in that congregation. Stefanus was at your side as he was going to be every Sunday after that for . . . how long?

HELEN. Five years.

MARIUS. Another five years. That was all a long time ago.

HELEN. More than a long time, Marius. It feels like another life. (*ELSA returns with a tray of tea and sandwiches.*)

MARIUS. Ah, here comes your supper. I must be running along.

ELSA. Just a sandwich, Dominee. Neither of us is very hungry.

MARIUS. I'll drop by tomorrow night after the service if that is alright with you, Helen. (*Collects his hat and scarf.*)

ELSA. Won't you have a cup of tea with us? It's the least we can offer in return for all those lovely vegetables.

MARIUS. Thank you, Miss Barlow, but I don't want to intrude. Helen tells me you're here for just the night. I'm sure you ladies have got things to talk about in private.

ELSA. We've already done quite a lot of that, haven't we, Helen? Please don't go because of me. I have some school work I must see to. I'll take my tea through to the back room.

HELEN. Don't go, Elsa!

ELSA. I told you I had papers to mark, Miss Helen. I'll just get on with that quietly while the two of you have a little chat.

HELEN. Please!

ELSA. Alright then, if it will make you happier I'll do my work in here.

MARIUS. No. I've obviously come at an inconvenient time.

ELSA. Not at all, Dominee. Miss Helen was expecting you.

(*Fetches the application form for the Old Age Home and hands it to Marius. A moment between ELSA and MARIUS. HE turns to Helen for confirmation.*)

HELEN. Yes, I was.

ELSA. How do you like your tea?

MARIUS. Very well, if you insist. Milk but no sugar. (*ELSA pours the tea. MARIUS hangs up his hat and scarf. There is an uncomfortable moment of silence. ELSA hands Marius his tea, leaves a cup on the table for Helen, takes a sandwich for herself, the tray and her tea and goes into the kitchen.*) You're quite certain you want to deal with this now, Helen?

HELEN. Yes, Marius.

MARIUS. It can wait until tomorrow.

HELEN. No, I'm ready. (*Sits at the table.*)

MARIUS. Right. Just before we start talking, Helen, the good news . . . (*ELSA tiptoes back from the kitchen into the bedroom alcove with her tea and begins to work on her papers. MARIUS hesitates for a moment and then resumes talking.*) The good news is that I've spoken to Dominee Gericke in Graaff-Reinet again and the room is definitely yours . . . that is, if you want it, of course. But they obviously can't have it standing empty indefinitely. As it is he's already broken the rules by putting you at the top of the waiting list, but it's a personal favor. He understands the circumstances. So the sooner we decide, one way or the other, the better. But I want you to know that I do realize how big a move this is for you. I want you to be quite certain and happy in your mind that you're doing the right thing. So don't think we've got to rush into it . . . start packing up immediately or anything like that. A decision must be made, one way or the other, but once you've done that you can relax and take all the time you need.

(*Spectacles, a little notebook, pen and pencil from a jacket pocket. The way he handles everything . . . care — and precisely . . . reveals a meticulous and orderly mind. HE opens the application form. MISS HELEN gives Elsa the first of many desperate and appealing looks. ELSA, engrossed in her work, does not apparently notice it.*)

HELEN. Marius, I just . . .

MARIUS. I know we went over this the last time, Helen, but there still are just a few questions. Yes . . . we put Stefanus' father's name down as Petrus Johannes Martins, but in the Church registry it's down as

Petrus *Jacobus. (Spectacles off.)* Which one is correct, Helen? Can you remember? You were so certain of the Petrus Johannes last time.

HELEN. I still am! But what did you say the other one was?

MARIUS. (*Holding the notebook up to the candlelight.*) Petrus Jacobus.

HELEN. Jacobus . . . Johannes . . . No, maybe I'm not sure.

MARIUS. In that case what I think I will do is just enter it as Petrus J. Martins. Just as well I checked. (*Spectacles on. Back to the form.*) And next . . . yes, the date of your confirmation. Have you been able to find the certificate?

HELEN. No, I haven't. I'm sorry, Marius. I have been looking but I'm afraid my papers are all in a mess.

MARIUS. (*Spectacles off.*) I've been through the Church records again but I can't find anything that sheds any light on it. It's not at all that important, of course, but it would have been nice to have had that date as well. (*Spectacles on.*) Let's see . . . what shall we do? You think you were about twelve at the time?

HELEN. Something like that.

MARIUS. What I'll do is just pencil in 1920 and have one more look. I hate giving up on *that* one. But you surprise me, Helen . . . of all dates to have forgotten. That takes care of the form now . . . (*His notebook.*) . . . Yes. Two little points from Dominee Gericke, after which you can relax and enjoy your supper. He asked me . . . and do believe me, Helen, he was only trying to be practical and helpful, nothing else . . . whether you had taken care of everything by way of a last will and testament, and obviously I said I didn't know.

HELEN. What do you mean, Marius?

MARIUS. That in the event of something happening, your house and possessions will be disposed of in the way that you want them to be. Have you done that?

HELEN. (*Taking a legal document out of the red box.*) I've still got a copy of Stefanus' will. He left everything to me.

MARIUS. We're talking about you, Helen. Have you seen a lawyer?

HELEN. No, I . . . I never thought of it.

MARIUS. Then it is just as well Dominee Gericke asked. Sit down, Helen. (*HELEN sits clutching the red box.*) Believe me, Helen, in my time as a minister I have seen so many bitterly unhappy situations because somebody had neglected to look after that side of things. Families not talking to each other! Law suits over a few sticks of furniture! I really do think it is something you should see to. We're at an age now when anything can happen. I had mine revised only a few months ago. (*His notebook.*) And finally, he made the obvious suggestion that we arrange for you to visit the Home as soon as possible. Just to meet the Matron and the other people there and to see your room. He's particularly anxious for you to see it so that you know what you need to bring on your side. He had a dreadful to-do there a few months ago with a lady who tried to move a whole houseful of furniture into her little room. Don't worry, there's plenty of space for personal possessions and a few of your . . . ornaments. That covers everything, I think. All that's left now is for you to sign it . . . provided you still want to do that, of course. (*Places his fountain pen in readiness on the form.*)

HELEN. (*Rises, trying to take command.*) Marius . . . please . . . please . . . can I talk for a little bit now?

MARIUS. But of course, Helen.

HELEN. I've been doing a lot of thinking since we last spoke . . .

MARIUS. Good! We both agree that was necessary. This is not a step to be taken lightly.

HELEN. Yes, I've done a lot of thinking and I've worked out a plan.

MARIUS. For what, Helen?

HELEN. A plan to take care of everything.

MARIUS. Excellent!

HELEN. I'm going in to Graaf-Reinet next week, Marius, to see a doctor. I'm going to make the appointment on Monday and I'll ask Gertruida to drive me in.

MARIUS. You make it sound serious, Helen.

HELEN. No, it's just my arthritis. I'm going to get some medicine for it.

MARIUS. For a moment you had me worried. I thought the burns were possibly more serious than we had realized. But why not save yourself a few pennies and see Dr. Lubbe at the Home? He looks after everybody there free-of-charge.

HELEN. (*Hanging on.*) And spectacles. I'm going to make arrangements to see an optician and get a pair of spectacles.

MARIUS. Splendid, Helen! You certainly have been making plans.

HELEN. And finally I've decided to get Katrina to come in two or three times a week to help me with the house.

(*Turns and looks at Elsa proudly. SHE is very pleased with herself.*)

MARIUS. Katrina?

HELEN. Little Katrina. Koos Magas' wife.

MARIUS. I know who you're talking about, Helen, it's just . . . Oh dear! I'm sorry to be the one to tell you this, Helen, but I think you are going to lose your little Katrina.

HELEN. What do you mean, Marius?

MARIUS. Koos has asked the Divisional Council for a transfer to their Aberdeen depot and I think he will get it.

HELEN. So . . .

MARIUS. I imagine Katrina and the baby will go with him.

HELEN. Katrina . . .

MARIUS. Will be leaving the village.

HELEN. No, it can't be.

MARIUS. It's the truth, Helen.

HELEN. But she's said nothing to me about it. She was here just a few days ago and she didn't mention anything about leaving.

MARIUS. She most probably didn't think it important.

HELEN. How can you say that, Marius? Of course it is! She knows how much I depend on her. If Katrina goes I'll be completely alone here except for you and the times when Elsa is visiting. (*MISS HELEN becomes increasingly distressed.*)

MARIUS. Come now, Helen! It's not as bad as that. I know Katrina is a sweet little soul and that you are very fond of her, as we all are, but don't exaggerate things. There are plenty of good women in the location who can come in and give you a hand in here and help you pack-up . . . if you decide to go. Tell you what I'll do . . . if you're worried about a stranger being in here with all your personal things. I'll lend you my faithful old Nonna. She's been looking after me for ten years now and in that time I haven't missed a thing. You could trust her with your life.

HELEN. I'm not talking about a servant, Marius.

MARIUS. I thought we were.

HELEN. Katrina is the only friend I've got left in the village.

MARIUS. That's a very hard thing you're saying, Helen. We all still like to think of ourselves as your friends.

HELEN. I wasn't including you, Marius. You're different. But as for the others . . . ? They've all become strangers to me. I might just as well not know their names. And they treat me as if I'm a stranger to them as well.

MARIUS. You're being very unfair, Helen. They behave towards you in the way you apparently want them to, which is to be left completely alone. Really Helen! Strangers? Old Gertruida, Sterling, Jerry, Boet, Mrs. van Heerden . . . ? You grew up in this village with all of them. To be very frank, Helen, it's your manner which now keeps people at a distance. I don't think you realize how much you've changed over the years. You're not easily recognizable to others anymore as the person they knew fifteen years ago. And then your hobby, if I can call it that, hasn't really helped matters. This is not exactly the sort of room the village ladies are used to, or would feel comfortable in having afternoon tea. As for all that out there . . . the less said about it the better.

HELEN. I don't harm or bother anyone, Marius!

MARIUS. And does anyone do that to you?

HELEN. Yes! Everybody is trying to force me to leave my home.

MARIUS. Nobody is trying to force you, Helen! In Heaven's name where do you get that idea from? If you sign this form it must be of your own free will. You're very agitated tonight, Helen. Has something happened to upset you? You were so reasonable about everything the last time we talked. You seemed to understand that the only motive on our side was to try and do what is best for you. And even then it's only in the way of advice. We can't *tell* you what to do. But if you want us to stop caring about what happens to you we can try . . . though I don't know how our Christian consciences will allow us to do that.

HELEN. I don't believe the others care about me, Marius. All they want is to get rid of me. This village has also changed over the past fifteen years. I don't recognize it anymore as the simple, innocent world I grew up in.

MARIUS. If it's as bad as that, Helen, if you are now really that unhappy and lonely here, then I don't think you should have any doubts about leaving.

(*MISS HELEN's emotional state has deteriorated steadily. Marius' fountain pen has ended up in her hand. SHE looks down at the application form . . . a few seconds pause and then a desperate cry.*)

HELEN. Why don't you stop me, Elsa! I'm going to sign it!

ELSA. (*Abandoning all pretense of being absorbed in her work.*) Then go ahead and do it! Sign that fucking form. If that's what you want to do with your life just get it over and done with, for God's sake.

MARIUS. Miss Barlow!

ELSA. (*Ignoring him.*) What are you waiting for, Helen? It's late and we want to go to bed.

HELEN. (*Runs over helplessly to Elsa.*) But you said I mustn't sign it.)

ELSA. (*Brutally.*) I've changed my mind. Do it. Hurry up and dispose of your life so we can get on with ours.

HELEN. Stop it, Elsa. Help me. Please help me.

ELSA. (*Attempting to put away her papers.*) Sorry, Helen. I've had more woman battering today than I can cope with. You can at least say No. That woman on the road couldn't. But if you haven't got the guts to do that, then too bad. I'm not going to do it for you.

HELEN. I tried.

ELSA. You call that trying? All it required was one word . . . "No."

HELEN. Please believe me, Elsa . . . I was trying!

ELSA. No good, Helen. If that's your best then maybe you will be better off in an old age home.

MARIUS. Gently, Miss Barlow! In Heaven's name gently! (*Back to Elsa.*) What's got into you?

ELSA. Exhaustion, Dominee. Very near total mental and emotional exhaustion to the point where I want to scream. I've already done that once today and right now I wouldn't mind doing it a second time. Yes, Helen, I've had it. Why were you "crying out to me in the dark?" To be an audience when you signed away your life? Is that why I'm here? Twelve hours of driving like a lunatic for that? God. What a farce! I might just as well have stayed in Cape Town.

(*Crosses into the lounge.*)

MARIUS. Maybe it's a pity you didn't. I think I understand now why Helen is so agitated tonight. Unfortunately you are here and if you've got anything to say to her in Heaven's name be considerate of the state she is in. She needs help, not to be confused and terrified even more.

ELSA. Helen understands the way I feel. We *did* do a lot of talking before you arrived, Dominee.

MARIUS. I'm concerned with *her* feelings, Miss Barlow, not yours. And if by any chance you are as well, then try to show some respect for her age. Helen is a much older woman than you. You were shouting at her as if she were a child.

ELSA. (*Enraged.*) Me, treating her like a child? Oh my God! You can stand there and accuse me of that after what I've just seen and heard from you?

MARIUS. I don't know what you're talking about.

ELSA. Then I'll tell you. You were doing everything in your power to bully and blackmail her into signing that form. You were taking the grossest advantage of what you call her confusion and helplessness. I've been trying to tell her she's neither confused nor helpless.

MARIUS. So you know what is best for her.

ELSA. No no no! Wrong again, Dominee. I think *she* does. And if you had given her half a chance she would have told you that that is not being dumped in an old-age home full of old people who have reached the end of their lives. She hasn't. You forget one thing: I didn't stop her signing that form. She stopped herself.

MARIUS. That was a moment of confusion.

ELSA. There you go again! Can't you leave that word alone? Helen is not confused!

MARIUS. When Helen and I discussed the matter a few days ago . . .

ELSA. Don't talk about her as if she's not here. She's sitting right over there. Ask her, for God's sake . . . but this time give her a chance to answer.

MARIUS. Don't try to goad me with blasphemy, Miss Barlow. I'm beginning to think Helen needs as much protection from you as she does from herself.

ELSA. You still haven't asked her.

MARIUS. Because I have some sympathy for her condition. Look at her! She is in no condition now, thanks to you, to think clearly about anything.

ELSA. She was an emotional mess, thanks to you, long before I opened my mouth. Don't expect me to believe you really care about her.

MARIUS. (*Trying hard to control himself.*) Miss Barlow, for the last time, what you do or don't believe is not of the remotest concern to me. Helen is, and my concern is that she gets a chance to live out what is left of her life as safely and as happily as is humanly possible. I don't think that should include the danger of her being trapped in here when this house goes up in flames.

ELSA. What are you talking about?

MARIUS. Her accident. The night she knocked over those candles. (*ELSA is obviously at a loss.*) You don't know about that? When was it, Helen? Four weeks ago? (*Pause . . . MISS HELEN doesn't respond.*) Helen? I see. You didn't tell your friend about your narrow escape. I think I owe you an apology, Miss Barlow. I assumed you knew all about it.

ELSA. You owe me nothing. Just tell me what happened.

MARIUS. Yes, it was about four weeks ago. Helen knocked over those candles and set fire to the curtains. I try not to think about what would have happened if Sterling hadn't been looking out of his window at that moment and seen the flames. He rushed over, and just in time. She had stopped trying to put out the flames herself and was just standing staring at them. Even so she picked up a few bad burns on her hands. We had to get Sister Lategan out of bed to treat them. But it could have been a lot worse. (*ELSA is staring at Miss Helen.*) We don't want that on our consciences. So you see Miss Barlow, our actions have not been quite as pointless or as uncaring as they must have seemed to you.

ELSA. One of the candles started smoking badly and there was a little accident at the stove while you were making prickly-pear syrup for me! Oh boy! . . . you certainly can do it, Helen. Don't let us ever again talk about trust between the two of us. Anyway, that settles it. I leave the two of you to fight it out . . . and may the best man win! I'm going to bed.

(*Goes to the bedroom alcove and pulls out a nightgown from her overnight bag.*)

HELEN. Give me a chance to explain.

ELSA. (*Ignoring the plea.*) Goodnight. See you in the morning. I'll be making an early start, Helen.

HELEN. Don't abandon me, Elsa!

ELSA. You've abandoned yourself, Helen! Don't accuse me of that! You were the first to jump overboard. You haven't got enough faith in your life and your work to defend them against him . . . You lie to me! . . . and such stupid bloody lies. What was the point? For that matter what was the point to anything? Why *did* you make me come up here? And then all our talk about trust! God, what a joke. You've certainly made me make a fool of myself again, but this time I don't think it's funny. In fact I fucking well resent it.

HELEN. I didn't tell you because I was frightened you would agree with them.

ELSA. Don't say anything more, Helen. You're making it worse. (*Studying Miss Helen with cruel detachment.*) But you might have a point there. Now that I've heard about your "little accident" I'm beginning to think they might be right. (*The room.*) Corrugated iron and wooden walls? Give it half a chance and this would go up like a bonfire. (*Hating herself, hurting herself every bit as much as she is doing to Helen but unable to stop.*) And he says you were just standing and staring at it. What was that all about? Couldn't you make a run for it? They say that about terror . . . either makes you run like hell or stand quite still. Sort of paralysis. Because it was just an accident, wasn't it, Helen? I mean, you weren't trying anything else were you? Spite everybody by taking the house with you in a final blaze of glory! Dramatic! . . . but it's a hell of a way to go. There are easier methods.

(*MISS HELEN goes up to Elsa and stares at her.*)

HELEN. Who are you? (*The question devastates ELSA.*)

MARIUS. (*Intercepting.*) Ladies . . . ladies . . . Enough! Stop now! I don't know what's going on between the two of you, but in Heaven's name stop it. (*ELSA goes into the bedroom alcove and sits on the bed. MARIUS goes to help MISS HELEN but SHE waves him aside and sits at the table. SHE quietly stares into the flame of the moon candle. MARIUS approaches Elsa.*) I think Helen is aware of the dangers involved, Miss Barlow. And now that you are as well, can't we appeal to you to add your weight to ours and help persuade her to do the right thing? As I am sure you now realize, our only concern has been her well-being.

ELSA. You want my help.

MARIUS. Yes. If now at last you understand why we were trying to persuade Helen to move to the Home, then on her behalf I am indeed appealing to you. We don't persecute harmless old ladies, Miss Barlow.

ELSA. And one that isn't so harmless?

MARIUS. Now what are you trying to say?

ELSA. That Helen isn't "harmless," Dominee. Anything but that. That's why you people can't leave her alone.

MARIUS. For fifteen years we have done exactly that.

ELSA. Stoning her house and statues at night is not leaving her alone. That is not the way you treat a "harmless" old lady.

MARIUS. In Heaven's name! Are you going to drag that up? Those were children, Miss Barlow, and it was all a long, long time ago. It has not happened again. Do you really mean to be that unfair? Can't you bring as much understanding as you claim to have of Helen's situation, to a few other things as well? You've seen what is out there . . . (*Gesture to the window and Miss Helen's "Mecca."*) How else do you expect the simple children of the village to react to all that? It frightens them, Miss Barlow. I'm not joking! Think back to your impressionable years as a little girl. I know for a fact that all the children in the village believe this house is haunted and that ghosts walk around out there at night. Don't scoff at them. I'm sure there were monsters and evil spirits in your childhood as well. But as I said, that was all a long, long time ago. The moment we discovered what they were doing we in turn did everything we could to put a stop to it. Mr. Lategan, the school principal and I, both lectured them in the sternest possible manner. Come now, Miss Barlow . . . have you learned nothing about us in the course of the few years that you've been visiting the village?

ELSA. A lot more than I would have like to. Those children didn't arrive at an attitude to Helen on their own. I've also heard about the parents who frighten naughty children with stories about Miss Helen's "monsters." Those children got the courage to start throwing stones because of what they had heard their mothers and fathers saying. And as far as *they* are concerned Helen is anything but a harmless old lady. God, what an irony. We spend our time talking about "poor, frightened Miss Helen" whereas it's all of you who are really frightened.

MARIUS. I can only repeat what I've already said to Helen: the people you are talking about grew up with her and have known her a lot longer than you. (*Crosses to the lounge.*)

ELSA. Not anymore. You also said that, remember. That stopped fifteen years ago when she didn't resign herself to being the meek, church-going little widow you all expected of her. Instead she did something which small minds and small souls can never forgive . . . she dared to be different! (*Following MARIUS into the lounge.*) Which does make you right about one thing, Dominee . . . those statues out there *are* monsters. And they are that for the simple reason that they express Helen's freedom. Yes, I never thought it was a word you would like, I'm sure it ranks as a cardinal sin in these parts. A free woman! God forgive us! Have you never wondered why I come up here? It's a hell of a long drive, you know, if the only reason is sympathy for a lonely lady who nobody is talking to anymore. And it's also not for the scenery. She challenges me, Dominee. She has challenged me into an awareness of myself and my life and my responsibilities to both that I never had until I met her. There's a hell of a lot of talk about freedom, and all sorts of it, in the world where I come from. But it's mostly talk, Dominee, easy talk and nothing more. Not with Helen. She's lived it. One dusty afternoon five years ago when I came walking down that road, hoping for nothing more than to get away from the flies that were driving me mad, I met the first truly free spirit I have ever known. (*Looking at Helen.*) And it is her betrayal of all of that tonight that has made me behave the way I have.

MARIUS. (*A pause before he speaks. HE has been confronted with something he has never had to deal with before.*) You call that . . . that nightmare out there an expression of freedom?

ELSA. Yes. Scary, isn't it? What did you call it earlier? Her hobby? (*Laughs.*) Oh no, Dominee. It's much more dangerous than that . . . and I think you know it.

MARIUS. In another age and time it might have been called idolatry.

ELSA. Did you hear that, Helen? (*To Marius.*) You know what you've just said don't you?

MARIUS. (*Total conviction.*) Oh yes . . . yes indeed I do. I am choosing my words very carefully, Miss Barlow. When I first realized that it was my duty as a friend and a Christian to raise the question with Helen of a move to an old age home, I decided I would do so on the basis of her physical well-being and safety and nothing else. Helen will tell you that that is all we have ever talked about. I came here tonight meaning once again to do only that. But you have raised other issues, chosen to talk about more than just that . . . which forces me now to do so as well. Because there is a lot more than Helen's physical well-being that has worried me, Miss Barlow . . . and gravely so! Those "expressions of freedom" have crowded out more than just a few fresh vegetables. I do not take them lightly anymore. I remember the first one very clearly, Helen. I made the mistake of smiling at it, dismissing it as an idle whim coming out of your loneliness. In fact I think that is how you yourself described it to me . . . as something to pass away the time. I was very wrong, wasn't I? . . . and very slow in realizing what was really happening. I only began to feel uneasy about it all that first Sunday you weren't in Church. The moment I stood up there in front of the congregation I knew your place was empty. But even then you see, I thought you were sick. After the service I hurried around here, but instead of being in bed there you were outside in the yard making yet another . . . (*At a loss for words.*) . . . I don't really know what to call them.

HELEN. (*A small but calm voice. She is very still.*) It was an owl, Marius. My first owl.

MARIUS. It couldn't have waited until after the service, Helen?

HELEN. Oh no! (*Quietly emphatic.*) The picture had come to me in here the night before. I just had to go to work immediately while it was still fresh in my mind. But don't ever think that missing Church that Sunday was something I did lightly, Marius. You don't break the habit of a lifetime without realizing that that life will never be quite the same again. I was dressed and ready! I had my Bible and Hymn Book, I was on the point of leaving this room as I had done every Sunday for as long as I could remember . . . but I knew that if I did, I would never make that owl . . .

MARIUS. Helen, Helen! I grieve for you! You turned your back on your Church, your faith and then on us, for that? Do you realize that that is why you are now in trouble and so helplessly alone? Those statues out there can't give you the love and take care of you the way we wanted to. And God knows we were ready to do that,

Helen. But you spurned us, you turned your back on our love and left us for the company of those cement monstrosities.

(*ELSA, who has been listening and watching quietly, begins to understand.*)

ELSA. Helen, listen to me . . . listen to me carefully . . . because if you understand what I'm going to say, I think everything will be alright. They're not only frightened of you, Helen, they're also jealous. It's not just the statues that frighten them. They were throwing stones at something much bigger than that . . . you. Your life, your beautiful light-filled glittering life. And they can't leave it alone, Helen, because they are so, so jealous of it. (*Sits on the chaise.*)

HELEN. (*Speaks calmly.*) Is that true, Marius?

MARIUS. Helen? Has your trust in me been eroded away to the extent that you can ask me that? Does she have so much power over you that you will now believe anything she says?

HELEN. Then . . . it isn't true?

MARIUS. Dear God . . . what is there left for me to say or do that will make you listen to me the way you do to her!

HELEN. But I have been listening to you, Marius.

MARIUS. No you haven't! If that were so you wouldn't be asking me to defend myself against the accusations of someone   who   knows   nothing . . . nothing! . . . about my true feelings for you. I feel as though I were on trial, Helen. For what? For caring about you? (*Confronting Helen.*) That I am frightened of what you have done to yourself and your life . . . Yes! That is true! When I find that the twenty years we have known each other, all that we have shared in that time, is outweighed by a handful of visits from her . . . then Yes again. That leaves me bewildered and jealous. Don't you realize that you are being used, Helen — she as much as admitted to that — to prove some lunatic notion about freedom? And since we're talking about it, Yes yet again! I *do* hate that word. You aren't free, Helen. If anything, exactly the opposite. Don't let her deceive you. If there is one last thing you will let me do for you let it be this . . . see yourself as I do and tell me if that is what you call "being free." A life I care about as deeply as any I have ever known, trapped now finally in the nightmare this house has become . . . with an illiterate little colored girl and a stranger from a different world as your only visitors and friends! I know I'm not welcome in anymore. I can feel it the moment I walk in. It's unnatural, Helen. Your life has become as grotesque as those creations of yours out there. Why, Helen? Why? I will take that question with me to my grave. What possessed you to abandon the life you had, your faith?

HELEN. What life, Marius? What faith? The one that brought me to Church every Sunday? (*Shaking her head.*) No. You were much too late if you only started worrying about that . . . on that first Sunday I wasn't there in my place. The worst had happened long, long before that. All those years when, as Elsa said, I sat there so obediently next to Stefanus, it was a terrible, terrible lie. I tried hard, Marius, but your sermons, the prayers, the hymns, they had all become just words. Do you know what the word "God" looks like when you've lost your faith? It looks like a little stone, a cold round little stone. "Heaven" is another one, but it's got an awkward, useless shape, while "Hell" is flat and smooth. All of them . . . damnation, grace, salvation . . . a handful of stones.

MARIUS. (*Sits next to Miss Helen.*) Why didn't you come to me, Helen! If only you had trusted me enough to tell me, and we had faced it together, I would have broken my soul to help you win back that faith.

HELEN. It was too late. I'd accepted it. Nothing more was going to happen to me except time and the emptiness inside and I had got used to that . . . until the night in here after Stefanus' funeral. (*Pause. MISS HELEN makes a decision.*) Do you remember it, Marius? You brought me home from the cemetery and after we had got inside the house and you had helped me off with my coat, you put on the kettle for a pot of tea and then . . . ever so thoughtfully! . . . pulled the curtains and closed the shutters. Such a small little thing, and I know you meant well by it, that you didn't want people to stare in at me and my grief . . . but in doing that it felt as if you were putting away my life as surely as the undertaker had done to Stefanus a little earlier when he closed the coffin lid. There was even an odor of death in here with us, wasn't there, sitting in the gloom and talking, both of us in black, our Bibles on our laps. Your words of comfort didn't help. But that wasn't your fault. You didn't know I wasn't mourning Stefanus' death. He was a good man, and it's very sad that he had died so young, but I never loved him. My black widowhood was really for my own life, Marius.

While Stefanus was alive there had at least been some pretense at it . . . of a life I hadn't lived, but with him gone . . . ! You had a little girl in here with you, Marius, who had used up all the prayers she knew and was dreading the moment when her mother would bend down, blow out the candle and leave her in the dark. You lit one for me before you left . . . there was a lot of darkness in this room! . . . and after you had gone I sat here with it. Such a sad little light, with its little tears of wax running down the side! I had none, neither for Stefanus nor myself. That little candle did all the crying in here that night, and it burnt down very low while doing that. I don't know how much time had passed while I just sat here staring into its flame . . . I had already surrendered myself to what was going to happen when it went out . . . but instead of it doing the same, allowing the darkness to defeat it, that small uncertain little light seemed to find its courage again. It started to get brighter and brighter, leading me, Marius. . . . a strange feeling it was leading me to a place I had never been before. (*Looks around the room and then speaks with quiet authority.*) Light the candles, Elsa. That one first. (*Indicating a candelabra that has been set up very prominently on an old trunk. Using a taper ELSA LIGHTS THE CANDLES on the trunk candelabra then gracefully continues around the room lighting the candles on the window sill, the shaker table and the top of the sideboard.*) . . . and you know why, Marius? That is the East. Go out there into the yard and you'll see that all my Wise Men and their camels are travelling in that direction. Follow that candle on and one day you'll come to Mecca. Oh yes, Marius, it's true! I've done it. That is where I went that night and it was the candle you lit that led me there. (*Radiantly alive with her vision.*)

A city, Marius! A city of light and color more splendid than anything I had ever imagined. There were palaces and beautiful buildings everywhere, with dazzling white walls and glittering minarets. Strange statues filled the courtyards. The streets were crowded with camels and turbaned men speaking in a language I didn't understand, but that didn't matter because I knew, oh, I just knew it was Mecca! And I was on my way to the grand temple. In the center of Mecca there is a temple, Marius, and in the center of the temple is a vast room with hundreds of mirrors on the walls and hanging lamps and that is where the Wise Men of the East study the celestial geometry of light and color. I became an apprentice that night. Light them all, Elsa, so that I can show Marius what I've learnt. (*ELSA does so, continuing around the lounge, bedroom alcove and the backrooms. For the first time we see the full magic and splendor of the room. MISS HELEN laughs ecstatically as SHE lights a taper and hold it up to Marius.*) Look, Marius! Look! Light. Don't be nervous. It's harmless. It only wants to play. That is what I do in here. We play with it like children with a magical toy that never ceases to delight and amuse. Light just one little candle in here, let in the light from just one little star and the dancing starts. (*LIGHTS the oil lamp on the post.*) I've even taught it how to skip around corners. Yes I have. When I'm in the dark and look in *that* mirror I can see *that* mirror, and in that one the full moon when it rises over the Sneeuberg *behind* my back! (*Triumphantly taking in the whole room. ELSA is sitting on the chaise.*) This is my world and I have banished darkness from it. It is not madness, Marius. They say mad people can't tell the difference between what is real and what is not. I can. I know my little Mecca out there, and this room, for what they really are. I had to learn how to bend rusty wire into the right shape and mix sand into cement to make my Wise Men and their camels, how to grind down beer bottles in a coffee mill to put glitter on my walls. My hands will never let me forget. They'll keep me sane. It's the best I could do, as near as I could get to the real Mecca. My journey is over now. This is as far as I can go. (*Hands back the applica-*

tion form to Marius.) I won't be using this. I can't reduce my world to a few ornaments in a small room in an old-age home.

(*MARIUS takes the form. When HE speaks again we sense a defeated man, an acceptance of the inevitable behind the quite attempt to maintain his dignity.*)

MARIUS. Mecca! So that's where you went. I'll look for it in my atlas of the world when I get home tonight. That's a long way away, Helen! I didn't realize you had travelled that far from me. So to find you I must light a candle and follow it to the East! (*A helpless gesture.*) No. I think I'm too old now for that journey . . . and I have a feeling that you will never come back.

HELEN. I'm also too old for another journey, Marius. It's taken me my whole life to get here. I know I've disappointed   you . . . most   probably   bitterly so . . . please believe me that it wasn't intentional. I had as little choice over all that has happened as I did over the day I was born.

MARIUS. You know something, Helen? I think I do believe you . . . which only makes it all the harder to accept. All these years it always felt as if I could reach you. It seemed so inevitable that I would . . . so right! That we should find each other again and be together for what time was left to us in the same world. It seems wrong . . . terribly wrong . . . that we won't. Aletta's death was wrong in the same way.

(*Pause. MARIUS tries to collect his spectacles and pens but falters.*)

HELEN. Marius?

MARIUS. I am trying to go. It's not easy . . . trying to find the first moment in a life that must be lived out in the shadow of something that is terribly wrong.

HELEN. We're trying to say goodbye to each other aren't we, Marius?

MARIUS. Yes, I suppose it has come to that. I never thought that was going to happen tonight but I suppose there *is* nothing else left to say. (*Collects his things, puts on his hat and scarf.*) Make sure all the candles are out when you go to bed, Helen. (*Pauses at the door.*) I've never seen you as happy as that! There was more light in you than in all your candles put together.

(*MARIUS leaves. A silence follows his departure, MISS HELEN puts out the oil lamp. ELSA eventually makes a move and starts blowing out the candles on the window sill and the shaker table.*)

HELEN. No, don't! I must do it.

(*From this point on MISS HELEN goes around the room putting out the candles — a quiet but deliberate and grave punctuation to what follows.*)

ELSA. Tell me about his wife.

HELEN. Her name was Aletta. Aletta Byleveld. I've only seen pictures of her. She must have been a very beautiful woman.

ELSA. What happened?

HELEN. Her death?

ELSA. Yes.

HELEN. All I know is that there was long illness. And a very painful one. They never had any children. Marius was a bitter and lonely man when he first came to the valley. Why do you ask?

ELSA. Because he was, and most probably still is, in love with you.

(*Fetches the tray from the kitchen and begins to clear the dishes off the table.*)

HELEN. Elsa?

ELSA. Yes. I don't suppose I would have ever guessed it if it hadn't been for tonight — like all good Afrikaners he does a very good job of hiding his feelings — but it is very obvious now.

HELEN. (*Agitated.*) Elsa, you're very wrong. When he used the word love he meant it in the way . . .

ELSA. No, Helen. I'm not talking about the good shepherd's feelings for one of his flock. Marius Byleveld, the man, loves you, Helen, the woman.

HELEN. No, No, No. Look at me, Elsa. Look at my hands.

ELSA. You fool! Do you think that is what we see when we look at you? You heard him: There is more light in you than all your candles put together. And he's right. You are radiant. You can't be that naive and innocent, Helen! (*MISS HELEN wants to deny it but the validity, the possible truth of what Elsa has said is very strong. ELSA puts the tray in the kitchen and crosses into the bedroom alcove.*) It's a very moving story. Twenty years of loving you in the disguise of friendship and professional concern for your soul. (*An unnatural and forced tone in her voice.*) Anyway that's his problem. Right, Helen? You did what you had to. In fact you deserve a few bravos for your performance tonight. And you did more than just say "no" to him. You affirmed your right . . . as a woman . . . (*Pause.*) Do you love him? The way he loves you?

HELEN. (*SHE thinks before speaking. When SHE does so there is no doubt about her answer.*) No, I don't.

ELSA. Just asking. You're also an Afrikaner. You could also be hiding your real feelings the way he did. That would make it an even better story! The two of you in this God-forsaken little village . . . each loving the other in secret!

(*Spitefully blows out two candles on the ledge in the alcove.*)

HELEN. Are you alright, Elsa?

ELSA. No.

HELEN. What's wrong?

ELSA. (*Crossing into the lounge.*) It's my turn to be jealous.

HELEN. Of what?

ELSA. (*Helpless gesture.*) Everything. You and him . . . and as stupid as it may sound I feel fucking lonely as well.

HELEN. You are jealous? Of us . . . Marius and me? . . . you with your whole life still ahead of you?

ELSA. Even that woman on the road has at least got a baby in her arms at this moment. She's got something, for Christ's sake. Mind you, it's cold out there now. That baby could be on her back again. She might have crawled out of her stormwater drain and started walking to keep warm.

HELEN. Leave that poor woman alone now, Elsa!

ELSA. She won't leave me alone, Helen!

HELEN. For all you know she might have got a lift.

ELSA. (*Another unexpected flash of cruelty.*) I hope not.

HELEN. (*Appalled.*) Elsa! That is not you talking. You don't mean that.

ELSA. Yes I do! A lift to where, for God's sake? There's no Mecca waiting for her at the end of that road, Helen. Just the rest of her life and there won't be any glitter on that. The sooner she knows what the score really is, the better.

HELEN. Then think about her baby, Elsa.

ELSA. What the hell do you think I've been doing? Do you think I don't care? That baby could have been mine, Helen! (*Pause. Sits at the table . . . then a decision.*) I may as well vomit it all out tonight. Two weeks after David left me I discovered I was pregnant. I had an abortion. (*Pause.*) Do you understand what I'm saying, Helen?

HELEN. I understand you, Elsa.

ELSA. I put an abrupt and violent end to the first real consequence my life has ever had!

HELEN. I understand, Elsa. (*Pause.*)

ELSA. There is a little sequel to my story about giving that woman a lift. After I stopped at the turn-off and she got out of the car, after I had given her what was left of my food and the money in my purse, after she had thanked me and told me over and over again that God would bless me . . . after all of that I asked her who she was. She said: My English name is Patience. She hitched up the baby, she tightened her doek, she picked up her little plastic shopping-bag and started walking. As I watched her walk away, measuring out the next eighty miles of her life in small steps, I wanted to scream. And about a mile further on—in the Kloof—I did exactly that. I stopped the car, switched off the engine, closed my eyes and started to scream. I screamed louder and longer than I have ever done in my life. I can't describe it, Helen. I hated her, I hated the baby, I hated you for dragging me all the way up here . . . and most of all I hated myself. That baby is mine, Helen. Patience is my sister, you are our mother . . . and I still feel fucking lonely.

HELEN. Then don't be so cruel to us. There were times tonight when I hardly recognized you. Why were you doing it?

ELSA. I want to punish us.

HELEN. For what?

ELSA. I've already told you. For being old, for being black, for being born . . . for being thirty-one years old and trusting enough to jump. For our stupid helplessness.

HELEN. You don't punish people for that Elsa. I only felt helpless tonight when I thought I had lost you.

ELSA. So what do you want me to do, Helen?

HELEN. Stop screaming.

ELSA. And cry instead?

HELEN. Why not? Is it something to be ashamed of? I wish I still could . . . not for myself . . . for you, for Patience, for her baby. Was it a boy or a girl?

ELSA. I don't know. I'll never know. (*Her moment of emotional release has finally come. SHE cries. MISS HELEN comforts her.*) I'll be alright.

HELEN. I never doubted that for a moment.

ELSA. (*Total exhaustion.*) God Almighty . . . what a day! I'm dead Helen . . . dead, dead, dead . . .

HELEN. No you're not. You're tired . . . and you've got every right and reason to be.

ELSA. I wasn't much of a help tonight, was I?

HELEN. You were more than that. You were a "challenge." I like that word.

ELSA. But we didn't solve very much.

HELEN. Nonsense! Of course we did. Certainly as much as *we* could. I *am* going to see a doctor and an optician and Katrina . . . (*Remembering.*) . . . or somebody else, will come in here a few times a week and help me with the house.

ELSA. My shopping list!

HELEN. It is as much as "we" could do, Elsa. (*Looking out at her yard.*) The rest is up to myself and, who knows . . . maybe it will be a little easier after tonight. I won't lie to you . . . I can't say that I'm not frightened anymore. But at the same time I think I can say that I understand something now. The road to my Mecca *was* one I had to travel alone. It was a journey on which no one could keep me company and because of that, now that it is over, there is only me there at the end of it. It couldn't have been any other way. You see, I meant what I said to Marius. This is as far as I can go. My Mecca is finished and with it . . . (*Pause.*) I must try to say it, mustn't I! . . . the only real purpose my life has ever had. (*Kneels down behind the trunk.*) I was wrong to think I could banish darkness, Elsa. Just as I taught myself how to light them, and what that means, I must teach myself now how to blow them out . . . (*Blows out the CANDLES on the trunk candelabra.*) . . . and what that means. (*Attempting a brave smile.*) The last phase of my apprenticeship . . . because if I can understand that, I'll be a master!

ELSA. I'm cold.

HELEN. (*Puts the blanket from the chaise around*

Elsa's shoulders.) Cup of tea to warm you up and then bed. I'll put on the kettle.

ELSA. And I've got just the thing to go with it. (*Goes into the bedroom alcove and returns with her toilet-bag from which she takes a small bottle of pills.*) Valiums. They're delicious. I think you should also have one.

HELEN. (*All innocence.*) So tiny! What are they? Artificial sweeteners?

(*The unintended and gentle irony of Miss Helen's question is not lost on ELSA. A little chuckle becomes a good laugh.*)

ELSA. That is perfect, Miss Helen. Yes, they're artificial sweeteners.

HELEN. I don't know how I did that, but that laugh makes me as proud of myself as any one of those statues out there.

(*MISS HELEN goes into the kitchen to put on the kettle. ELSA goes to the window and looks out at "Mecca." MISS HELEN returns.*)

ELSA. Helen, I've just had an idea. I think I know the cause of all your trouble. You've never made an angel.

HELEN. Good Heavens no. Why should I?

ELSA. Because I think they would leave you alone if you did.

HELEN. Bethesda doesn't need more of those, Elsa. The cemetery is full of them . . . all wings and halos, but no glitter. (*Her tongue-in-cheek humor.*) But if I did make one, it wouldn't be pointing up to heaven like the rest.

ELSA. No? What would it be doing?

HELEN. Come on, Elsa, you know! I'd have it pointing to the East. Where else? I'd misdirect all the good Christian souls around here and put them on the Road to Mecca. (*THEY both have a good laugh.*)

ELSA. God I love you! I love you so much it hurts.

HELEN. What about trust? (*Pause. The TWO WOMEN look at each other.*)

ELSA. Open your arms and catch me! I'm going to jump.

CURTAIN

COSTUME LIST

MISS HELEN:
    Distressed mauve cotton dress
    Distressed peach crocheted cardigan
    Brown leather sandals
    Grey wig

ELSA BARLOW:
    Pale blue plaid cotton shirt
    Olive drab cotton trousers
    White cotton tank top
    Brown leather sandals
    Bra
    Underpants
    Gold post earrings

    Onstage change:
    Patterned silk robe
    Grey cotton drawstring sweatpants
    Grey cotton sweatsocks

    Added for Act 2:
    Ecru crocheted sweater
    Distressed white Keds sneakers

MARIUS BYLEVELD:
    Two piece dark navy/black suit
    Grey and white stripe shirt
    Brown wool sweater vest
    Grey with green stripe tie
    Brown cotton socks
    Black oxfords
    Grey fedora
    Mauve knit scarf with fringe
    Black suspenders

Stage Preset

On Oriental Table:
    Candle in glass faceted holder
    Box of colorful mosaic chips (on floor)
On Chaise:
    Fine blue wool blanket
    Large cushion
    Pillow and blanket in disarray
On Window Ledge:
    Candle in a jar
    Pair of candlesticks
On Shaker Table:
    Taper holder with tapers
    Box of matches
    Cup of sand
    Dirty cup and saucer
    Candle in brass holder
    Two candles with hurricane cover
On Sideboard:
    Top Shelf:
    Candelabra with four candles
    Two candles in glass jars
    Assorted ornaments

    Bottom Shelf:
    Five candles in glass jars
    Candle in brass holder with moon cutout
    Box of matches
    Terra cotta carafe filled with water
    Glass
    Small bucket of sand
    Assorted ornaments
On Table:
    Dirty cup, saucer and teaspoon

Small plate with pieces of a sandwich
Red box open with letters askew
Sunshine Home brochure and application
Will

Around Table:
  Three chairs;   Middle Sideboard drawer filled with
    papers on the Stage Left chair
  Miss Helen's cardigan and some old rags on back of
    the Up Center chair
  Miss Helen's sandals under the table
On Post:
  Oil lamp with hurricane cover
  Brass candle snuffer
  Small mirror
On Washstand:
  Washbowl
  Pitcher of cool water in washbowl
  Soapdish
  Candle in brass holder
  Towel bar
  Foot stool (under washstand)
  Stool (Down Stage of washstand)
On Kitchen Window Ledge:
  Small candle in brass holder
  Pair of candlesticks
  Assorted ornaments
On Bed:
  Assorted cushions
—On Window Ledges over the Bed:
  Five candles in assorted terra cotta and glass jars
  Assorted ornaments
On Mecca Trunk:
  Candelabra with four candles
  Three votive candles

Taper
Coverlet
In Kitchen:
  On Top Shelf:
  Large Kettle of water on hotplate
  Small Kettle of water
  Teapot
  Potholder
  Jar with teaspoons
  Slop bowl
  Tea strainer
  Milk pitcher with lace cover
  Sugar bowl with lace cover
  Tin of tea
  Two cups and saucers
  Small plate with six biscuits

  On Bottom Shelf:
  Cutting Board
  Small plate
  Bread knife
  Butter knife
  Tin with eight slices of bread
  Jar of jam
  Three cups and saucers
  Serving Tray

  On Floor:
  Bucket for waste water
On Floor near the Chaise:
  Elsa's overnight bag with:
  Toilet kit containing—
    Jar of face cream
    Bottle of lotion
    Toothbrush

Toothpaste
Elastic hair bands
Hairbrush
Chapstick
Pill bottle with "Valiums"
Clothing—
   Socks
   Sweatpants
   Sneakers
   Nightgown
Elsa's briefcase with:
   Letter from Miss Helen
   Red marking pens
   Folder containing school papers
Elsa's sweater on top of bags
Hanging Fixtures:
   Chandelier over table
   Hanging lamp over sideboard
   Hanging lamp in bedroom alcove
   Wall sconce
   Hanging lamp in back room
   Hanging lamp in kitchen
Off Stage Right Preset:
   Sunglasses
   Keys
   Wicker basket with potatoes, tomatoes and beets
   Fountain pen
   Mechanical pencil
   Small leather notebook
   Spectacles and case
Off Stage Left Preset:
   Box with scented soap bars
   Towel
   Washcloth
   Robe

SET DRESSING NOT INCLUDED IN THE STAGE PRESET LIST:

— Statues by the porch
— Wheelbarrow filled with beer bottles inside the enclosed porch
— Chair with oriental robe thrown on it in the backroom
— Low table with assorted ornaments in the backroom
— Wicker basket filled with glass beads on the floor Downstage of the day bed
— A runner and throw rug in the hallway, an oriental area rug under the table and chairs and a throw rug next to the chaise
— Assorted mirrors on walls
— Brass wind chime in hallway, wood and glass bead wind chime in hallway and wood wind chime in backroom
— Sunburst cutout on porch
— Brass bell wind chime hanging inside the enclosed porch
These items can be incorporated into the stage preset if needed.

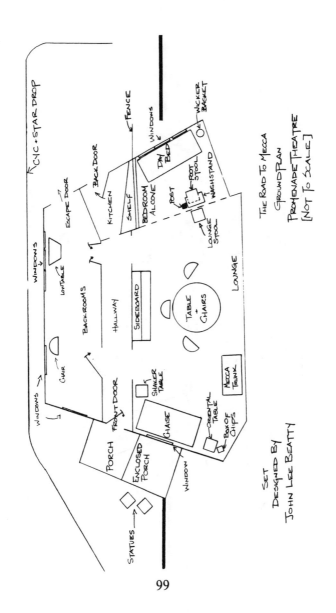

CYC + STAR DROP

WINDOWS

FENCE

BACK DOOR

ESCAPE DOOR

KITCHEN

SHELF

BEDROOM ALCOVE

DAY BED

WICKER BASKET

POST

FOOT STOOL

WASHSTAND

LOUNGE STOOL

WINDOWS

LOW TABLE

BACK ROOMS

HALLWAY

SIDEBOARD

TABLE + CHAIRS

LOUNGE

CHAIR

WINDOWS

FRONT DOOR

SHAKER TABLE

MECCA TRUNK

ORIENTAL TABLE

CHAISE

BOX OF CHIPS

PORCH

ENCLOSED PORCH

WINDOW

STATUES

THE ROAD TO MECCA
GROUND PLAN
PROMENADE THEATRE
[NOT TO SCALE]

SET
DESIGNED BY
JOHN LEE BEATTY

99

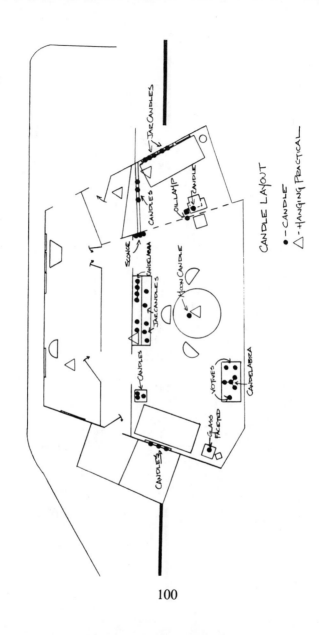

CANDLE LAYOUT

● - CANDLE

△ - HANGING PRACTICAL